Owen rested his hands against the boulder, waiting. The riders were mounting the trail. He heard voices, the creak of gear, the nearing clatter of iron on rock. He could not see them yet for the overhang. When the drift of noise grew directly beneath, he looked down and saw the first rider draw into view.

He gripped the boulder, lifted it; so suddenly that its mass tumbled outward, he lost balance and had to scramble back. He heard it strike; a horse screamed and plunged off the ledge; the thin, wailing cry of its rider died away into the gulf. The boulder made a falling crash that drowned all other sound— a thinning rattle of gravel, silence.

Owen saw none of it. Sweating and shaking, he stood and bawled down, "Keep your distance, you bastards!" There was no reply, only a faint murmur of talk and more silence. They would not dare come on . . . for a while . . .

Gunswift

by T. V. Olsen

A FAWCETT GOLD MEDAL BOOK

FAWCETT PUBLICATIONS, INC., GREENWICH, CONN.

MEMBER OF AMERICAN BOOK PUBLISHERS COUNCIL, INC.

ONE

A chill wind had dipped off the peaks, and Owen reached automatically for the long-gone buttons of his tattered sheepskin, and then remembering, dropped his hand back to the rifle across his knees. He hunched his chin into his collar and settled back on his heels, patient again. He was crouched in the heavy timber that mantled the slope shouldering steeply above the dry wash below. The camp down there was silent and deserted, as it had remained throughout this long afternoon of waiting.

Owen reflected for the hundredth time on the personality of the unseen camper. It was a small, Spartanly furnished outfit. Gear was piled neatly to one side, the embers of the dead fire had been carefully trod into the earth. An efficient man, no doubt a cautious one. Owen would have to set this up carefully in any case; he wanted his man alive.

He lifted his gaze to the opposite slope. Also heavily wooded, it afforded good cover for Abner. Two hours before, Owen had watched Ab take a position behind a screen of brush a few yards above the wash, had seen no movement from there since. These were two patient men who had traveled too long and far, on a quest that had settled into plodding habit, to come this near and lose their quarry. From far up the wash Owen heard the steady, monotonous creak of the sluice box. The sun had westered beyond the peaks; even the long afterlight was dimming. Garvey would soon quit for the day and return to camp.

The plan was simple. Owen and Abner had devised it

when they'd arrived here at midafternoon and spotted the layout. Without catching sight of Garvey, they picked out the sound of his workings, evidently on a running stream that branched off about this dry lower wash. The old man in the village had told them that Garvey was jumpy and spark-tempered; he'd struck a rich gold vein here a month ago, had shot at several people who'd ventured too near his claim. Garvey carried a revolver and rifle at all times, could use both.

"Friends of his?" the old man had asked; "We know him," had been Owen's meager reply. He smiled grimly now. They knew him . . . though only Abner had set eyes on him—that once and briefly, seven years ago. They knew his place and year of birth, his detailed description, his several occupations; they almost knew the hour of his death, Owen thought savagely. He considered that with merciless detachment: the thought was part of a pattern instilled in his mind.

Any chance sound in stealing up on the man would give them away; with his nerves at hair-trigger, Garvey would surely panic and begin shooting. With two of them in cover when Garvey returned to his camp, they could catch him close and between them, giving time for one to wing him if he cut down on the other. Owen hoped the man would have the sense to stand steady when he gave the order. . . .

Abruptly Owen's senses sharpened, straining to alertness. The wooden squeak of the sluice box had ceased. He cocked his head, listening, watching upwash through the dappling of foliage that concealed him.

Soon Garvey swung into view from around a crook in the steep banks. Now at close range, Owen gave him a raking scrutiny. A small and bearded man with faded eyes in a face as bland and unassuming as a tired sheep's, he wore filth-ingrained butternut pants and a sweat-clinging linsey-woolsey shirt, slouch hat pulled low. His narrow shoulders were stooped from his cramped labors. In one hand swung a rifle; in the other an elk-hide gold pouch.

He walked to the dead fire, bent to lay the pouch on

the ground and lean the rifle across it. He reached for a tier of stacked brush to start his supper fire. Owen stirred to ease his cramped legs muscles, then started to rise, hauling in breath to call sharp warning.

He froze with knees bent as Garvey suddenly stood. Watched, breath held, as the man raised his arms in a tremendous yawn and at the same time slowly turned to face the slope. For a moment Garvey's gaze swung and held on the spot where Owen crouched; then it moved idly on. Owen watched narrowly as the man bent again. But it was only to pick up his rifle and a bucket, then turn and tramp unhurriedly back up the wash beyond sight.

Owen sank down, his muscles trembling. A trickle of sweat cut raggedly down his ribs beneath his shirt. *Damn, he couldn't have seen me. Or did he? He'd started to lay a fire. . . . No, he needs water is all. Coffee.* Yet he wished he hadn't hesitated, that he had laid down his warning at once while Garvey's rifle was on the ground.

Seconds dragged into minutes, touching a wary unease to Owen's spine. The stream was only around the bend yonder. *Maybe he saw you then. Can't chance he'll run out.*

Owen unbent to slow erectness, scanning the wash and the silent flanking forest. Standing, he was a man of well above six feet, muscled like a blacksmith, his great-shouldered frame made bulkier by the heavy sheepskin. The hamlike hands gripping the rifle were scarred at the knuckles; his face was broad through the cheekbones with a nose twice broken, a face battered without being brutal—legacy of the fights and brawls that gravitated to a big, prideful man in this raw country. His shaggy hair sworled into a short chestnut beard that slurred the sharp angles of the lower part of his face. His eyes redeemed an allover roughness, being a clear, wide-open gray, yet mature and watchful to soberness.

About to call softly to Abner, he checked himself at a crackling of brush upslope, perhaps fifty yards to his rear. The noise abruptly stilled, as though the stalker had alarmed himself. *That was no animal,* Owen thought. *He saw me, must think I'm here to deadfall him for his poke. He won't run, leave that dust. He's circling behind to get a shot.* Motionless, he listened. For another telltale sound. When it came—the sharp snap of a foot-pressed twig—Owen left cover and went up the steep incline, toes digging hard at loam. Yet his great body moved with catfooted silence between the crowding tree boles.

He caught a glimpse of Garvey's narrow figure coming downslope, head lowered as he ducked through swatches of brush. Owen hugged a thick pine trunk, barely exposing his face as Garvey beat his way closer. Then the man spotted him, froze in his tracks.

Owen hauled in breath, released it in a shout: "Throw your guns away, Garvey. I don't want your dust, only—"

Garvey gave a sharp, shrinking cry, brought up his rifle with the quickness of thought. Its roar buffeted echoes from trees and rocks. The slug cascaded dead bark from the pine six feet above Owen's head and whined off at an angle. Garvey pivoted and lunged up the slope and Owen bounded after him, crashing like an angry bull through the thickets. He'd had a clear aim there, but no time for a wing shot. The desperate need to take Garvey alive burned in his chest like a bitter prayer.

The slope sheered to an ever-mounting pitch. Pine and brush growth ended just ahead, where Garvey was scrambling up a broken shale escarpment, leaping from one shattered boulder to the next in a goatlike desperation. Then the man lost balance, spun on his heel to grab at a splintered protuberance. He recovered footing, but lost his rifle. It slid and clattered down the face-rock, and fell at Owen's feet as he broke from brush and halted at the base, head tipped back. Garvey clung to the jut of the rock. He gibbered unintelligible curses.

"Come off there, Garvey!"

For answer Garvey reached a trembling hand to his pistol. Owen drew a breath and held it as he swung up his rifle and steadied a bead. He squeezed off the shot as Garvey's gun cleared leather. Garvey howled and sank down on his haunches, cradling his shattered arm. He let out a kind of wailing moan and subsided to frightened silence as Owen began swinging up the escarpment. He stepped carefully from one rock to the next, working his way at a cautious angle. He wanted to circle above Garvey and down to him.

But the prospector saw his intention. He scrambled higher, the panicked drive of his legs rattling down a small avalanche. Owen cursed once under his breath. Then he climbed, doggedly and furiously, to take advantage of every seam and outthrust on the escarpment's upper height. Garvey needed both hands; one was useless. His panting sobs drifted down to Owen, steadily closing the distance between them.

Garvey achieved a narrow ledge, his pain-drawn face peering over its brink. Then he ducked back. Owen halted, hearing Garvey's straining gasps and the grate of rock on rock. No time to move aside, time for nothing but to shrink helplessly against the cliffside as a huge chunk of shale toppled over the ledge rimrock. Deflected by a bulge, it veered aside and bounded past Owen by a full yard.

Pebbles and rock dust sifted over Owen; he coughed and choked back a momentary paralysis. Leaning out far as he dared, he gripped a fissured crack in the wall. He caught sight of a fresh foothold and swung himself sidelong to safety from well beneath the ledge.

Garvey appeared on the brink, a hefty piece of rock in his hand. He heaved it wildly and it harmlessly lobbed far out. He picked up another. The second throw shattered against rock so near Owen's body he felt the explosion of rotted shale bite into his sheepskin.

Owen had left his rifle below. He slipped out his Colt and fired. The slug burst the rimrock like a miniature grenade. Garvey faded quickly back from view. Owen sheathed the Colt and resumed climbing. Hot breath rasped in his throat and he was drenched with sweat. Pain needled his side.

Inside of a minute he reached a point horizontal with the ledge, then worked carefully toward it. Garvey sank on his haunches, holding his useless arm, and apathetically watched Owen's progress. Then he dropped his gaze to a point between his knees and did not look up until the big man dropped onto the ledge.

Owen caught him by the scruff of the neck, and with an effortless twist, brought him to his feet. His face shoved close to Garvey's sweat-shining one.

"Look at my face. You've seen it."

Against the choking grip Garvey stirred his head in dull negation. "No . . . never saw you. Never done you dirt."

"You've seen it." To his own ears, Owen's words were a dogged chant. "There were four others somewhat like it . . . a man, a woman . . . two girls not out of their teens. Think back . . . seven years ago . . . the blue-grass country outside Lexington. A big farm. You were with Tierney's Raiders. Only five of you left, rest wiped out by Morgan's Rifles. The war was a week over. . . ." He paused, seeing the pale terror mottle Garvey's blood-choked face. But the man's look was blank, half-comprehending.

"Or wouldn't you remember?" Owen went on softly. "There must have been a lot of burned farms . . . a lot of butchered women and children before the war's end, and after—for you and Tierney, eh? This was the Rutledge place. I'm Owen Rutledge. Those four people . . . my mother, my father, *my sisters, Garvey!*"

On the heel of his teeth-ground words, Owen's arm lifted and flung the man against the cliffwall. Garvey dropped to his hands and knees. His eyes glittered up through the lank hair falling over his eyes. "You . . ." he whispered, "you follered me all these years . . . all this way—"

"You're not finished till I am," Owen said tonelessly. "Two of the other raiders were killed, shot down by Federal troops. That left three—you, a lieutenant called Sykes, and Tierney himself. The three of you escaped to Texas and broke up." Owen towered above the man, his fists closing and unclosing. "Where are they, Garvey? Where are Tierney and Sykes, damn you!"

"Listen," Garvey pleaded hoarsely. "I tell you—we'll make a bargain—"

Owen bent and caught him by the throat, shaking him like a rat. "Slow or fast, Garvey. It's all one to me. Not to you." He let up the pressure of his thumbs to let Garvey suck wind into his bruised throat. He had to bend low to catch the ragged gasp: "Blanco. Blanco town . . . Blanco Basin. Both—of them."

Owen let go of him and stood, breathing heavily with the quick drain of tension. Seven years, he thought. Seven years . . . and now. . . . Strange how revenge thoughts grew to habit so dulled that a man could not yet be aware of the sharp exultance of journey's end. As though its end were the end of everything . . .

A deep voice hailed from below. Owen's back was toward the rimrock and he half-turned to glance down. He saw Abner at the cliff base, looking up with questioning concern. Owen waved an arm in reassurance.

He sensed rather than heard Garvey's sudden shift of movement, and swung back even as Garvey, rearing up on his knees in a burst of vitality, thrust his palm against Owen's middle and threw his weight behind it. The shove was a little thing to a man of Owen Rutledge's bulk —but with less than a foot of rimrock at his heels he could not step back for balance. For a moment he teetered wildly, tried to swing his weight to crash on his side. But most of his body plunged over the drop-off.

His fingers taloned against the rotted shale, caught his full weight with a violence that almost ripped his nails out. Rock crumbled beneath his fingers. They took fresh hold and he hung straight-armed, clinging along the outer ledge with his upper body hugging the rough rock, legs dangling free. He swung them inward for foothold and found none.

Garvey laughed hysterically. His boots rasped across the ledge. Owen flung back his head, saw the man above raise a boot to heel down on his hands.

The rifle made a clean, splitting report.

Garvey jerked and turned slowly in mid-stride with an arching grace. He pitched out over the rim in a twenty-foot free fall before his body crashed against the cliff's slow incline. Limply he rolled and bounded downward and was brought up, twisted and broken, across a base boulder.

Craning his head over his shoulder, Owen looked down. Abner lowered his rifle. "You got to hang on a bit there!" he boomed.

"A minute," Owen gasped. "No . . . longer . . . Ab."

He heard the quick shuffle and rattle of Abner's ascent. *He's coming too slow,* Owen thought almost detachedly, *but how fast can a man climb?* His arms numbed into his shoulders against his pendant weight, but shot into his fingers with raw pain where they curved into the ledge. He bent his head against the rock, eyes squeezed shut. Sparks flailed behind his lids. He knew his fingers were unbending. Then powerful hands fastened on his wrists.

He strained his neck backward, staring into Abner's mahogany-brown face. "Can't help you . . . no footing."

"You got to help me, Mars' Owen." The big Negro's voice held a positive calm. "Can't git no great leverage this way. I kin pull you a foot or so. You gits yore legs up far enough to dig in yore toes, I kin reach further, git a better grip. You ready?"

Owen jerked his head.

Abner heaved backward, squatted on the rim with his heels set. Owen felt his body rasp a foot upward along the rough shale. He flexed his knees, doubling his legs till he could hook his toes in a crevice against the ledge's underside.

"Got it," he panted.

Abner released one of his wrists, reached down long fingers to close on Owen's arm at the elbow. When his grip was firm he took like hold on the other arm. "Now you climb, man!"

Abner threw back his weight on his straining arms and Owen scrambled up the rimrock, toppled onto the ledge across Abner's legs. Then they lay, drawing great breaths.

Abner climbed to his feet and helped Owen up. "All right, Mars' Owen?"

Owen massaged his arms and shoulders, nodded numbly.

"He say anythin'?"

"Blanco . . . Blanco Basin."

"Which 'un?"

"Both. Tierney and Sykes. Both of them."

For a moment they simply stood looking into each other's faces. They had come a long way together—two men of two races with a single purpose. Watching the Negro with quiet affection, Owen thought of the marks these years and far driftings had left on them both. Abner was thirty-five—only six years Owen's senior—but the tight-kinked hair already lay gray and grizzled against his round head. They were equally thick-bodied, solid men in soiled, well-worn clothes, but Owen stood a full head taller than his companion.

Abner's deep, rich bass put into words their common, sobering thought. "Mighta lied, this Garvey-man. Cornered like you had him. Might not a knowed their whereabouts a-tall."

"Only one way to learn that," Owen said grimly.

Abner nodded once more, and gravely. "Best we see now to gittin' us off this rock, Mars' Owen."

TWO

Trouble, O Lawd! Nothin' but trouble
In de land o' Canaan—

Abner song-chanted softly as they rode between the slopes of a deep saddle between two mountain flanks. The pass bore the sign of old wagon passage and should bring them into Blanco Basin by nightfall.

"Very apt selection," Owen observed. "Got your juju, I hope?"

Abner's fist dipped inside his shirt collar and reappeared, holding up a bare-worn and desiccated rabbit's foot on a rawhide thong. "I been rubbin' her smart enough to drive Satan offn his hearth."

"You had her smoking for sure," Owen smiled.

Abner's broad palm cradled the rabbit's foot tenderly. "Best *gris-gris* in Kentucky. Sure-hell best in this lowdown West. Got it from Tante Marie day you was born, Mars' Owen."

Owen gave a sober and expectant nod, though he'd heard the story many times. Tante Marie had been his mother's personal maid and his own nurse for many years—an ancient, tiny Negress regarded by the blackfolk as the best voodoo woman in the country.

Abner went on distantly, "She say that day, 'You gwine be this white boy's bodyservant, little Ab. He be born to trouble, this little 'un. This *gris-gris* gwine protect you both. Day it's broken'll be day you die. Take care you never let it off your person.' "

Owen grinned, letting the old memories relax his taut senses. Memories of good days . . . yet Tante Marie had been right and he'd been born to trouble. Trouble that had begun for the South with that first shell on Sumter, that had never ended for him.

He and Abner had buried Garvey where they had caught up with him, rock-shoring the shallow grave against predators, and lashing two sticks crosswise for an anonymous marker. A week's travel northward had brought them below the broken dragon-spine of a minor arm of the Sangre de Cristo peaks, beyond which lay Blanco Basin. By this midafternoon, they were high on the south slopes of the saddle pass.

Abner called attention to the bleak, low-banked clouds scudding the north horizon. "They be on us in a couple hours, Mars' Owen. Be one hell of a big blow. We best take to shelter 'fore then."

"No shelter here. We'll push on. Land dips off from here. Make the low country before dark . . . if the storm holds off."

Abner nodded his tacit understanding of the other's bitter impatience. Strange, Owen reflected, how the pattern of seven years' quest became part of a man's very marrow, till many times it seemed a life-purpose in itself, at other times an insidious poison he knew he should shake for his own good . . . yet through it all, he'd kept an iron patience. Now, with the end in sight, he chafed against even a few hours' delay.

The first dip of land was gradual, the terrain bland enough to allow a fine-controlled clip. They paused often to blow their horses in this high, thin air. Blanco Basin's sprawling acreage grew to view below, a great grazing bowl tucked in a wild off-pocket of the Sangres. Here an outpost of civilization, a well-settled cattle country, had developed and prospered during two hundred years of Spanish and American rule, preserved by natural insulation from the brawling frontier outside. From this height through the amazingly clear and wine-sharp air, they made out the tidy sprawl of the town of Blanco far below.

The storm did not hit till they came off the pass into the first gentle foothills beneath, the pre-storm murk mingling with early dusk. Then it began, shortly buffeting men and horses in torrential sheets. Owen and Abner rode hugging the base of a high ridge, hoping for a cave or ledge that would afford shelter. They entered a cottonwood grove which broke the force of wind and rain as they headed into its murky aisles.

The forest floor was brush-free, so they caught the ruddy glow of a fire ahead while they were still a good fifty yards from it. Neither man said a word, nor slackened his pace. They'd faced too many dangers in harness for need of words. Though few would turn away a traveler on this wet and miserable night, the fire might belong to friend or foe. Owen knew the Negro's thought would be as his; Abner's silent action as he unbuttoned his mackinaw and loosened his Bowie knife in its sheath was expected. He carried no pistol, but he could throw or close-wield that heavy blade with equal dexterity.

Nearing the fire, Owen saw it situated back beneath a granite shelf protruding from the ridge face. Now a man stepped to the rim of firelight and peered through the rain-lashed dimness. His sharp call was razored with warning:

"Name yourselves, you out there!"

"Friends," Owen answered.

"Move in slow, friends."

Owen paced the bay into the tawny glow, reining in just beneath the overhang. He swung down and threw reins. The narrow man silhouetted against the fire was faceless as he stood hands on hips. He whistled, head tilting up and down to take Owen in. "Gawd, what a big ugly stud. All right, walk on in."

Owen came to the fire with a stiff-legged gait, giving only a glance and a nod to the other men sitting back against the rock wall, bending then to spread his chilled hands to the fire.

"A black stud, too. We're in fine company, Missou."

This from the narrow man. Owen turned to see him regarding Abner's dismount. The man glanced back at Owen, flamelight catching full on his face. He was hatless, his hair of flaxen paleness. His thin face was satyr-like, the eyebrows lighter than its sun-boiled ruddiness. Eyes of a deceptively weak and faded blue didn't lessen an impression of viciousness in leash. A low-thonged gun was strapped over his denims. *A pure-quill bad actor,* Owen thought.

The other man rose to his feet with the fluid grace of youth. "Couldn't expect a lowdown pilgrim that travels with his like to have the decency not to come to a white folks' camp."

Owen met the boy's challenging stare with unblinking calm. He was of middle height, sturdy of build in well-worn range clothes, his gaunt young face topped by black, curly hair, lending a certain rakishness that yet held no self-conscious swagger. The rash challenge in his words blended with a touchy pride of upbringing. The kid had seen enough of life to be self-sufficient without false cockiness, Owen guessed, but a streak of untempered wildness held him short of maturity.

"An ugly night," Owen said mildly. "We're cold and wet and obliged to you."

His moderate reply seemed to disconcert the boy; he glanced uncertainly at Abner, then at the narrow man who thinly smiled and shrugged one shoulder.

Abner broke the afterdrift of sudden silence: "I'll offsaddle, Mars' Owen, then rustle up more dry wood."

The boy's tense pose relaxed. He laughed. "Your man, eh? That's different. Good old-fashioned darky, are you, uncle?"

Abner had swung to Owen's horse; his hands halted on the latigo. He lazily glanced at the kid, his deep voice softly slurred: "Whose brother is I, boy? Mammy's or Pappy's?"

The kid made a choking sound. His hand moved; not quite touching the holster of his sidearm. Abner's right hand went under his coat to the unseen knife. Both were motionless, stare fixing stare. Owen stepped quietly back to stand by the narrow man, clearing the space between. He and Abner had been through this situation many times; however it went, he knew Abner would handle it for the best. He wouldn't take a hand unless the kid's companion did.

The narrow man sized this up with the tough, shrewd caution of an old hand. "Kid," he said tonelessly. "I'd let it ride."

Firelight flashed against the boy's eyes. He said, "A-a-h-h-" with a fathomless disgust and flung himself back on his blankets. *He's not afraid and he has good sense,* Owen thought. And knew a sudden perverse liking for this boy just as, at first sight, he'd instinctively disliked the narrow man. Owen made swift first judgments, and rarely had cause to regret them.

Abner toted their saddles and gear to the sheltered rear of the overhang, ground-haltered the horses to one side. Then he vanished in the outer darkness. Owen stood by the fire and shed his drenched clothes. The narrow man stared at his great-muscled height and laughed. "Damn, I never did see such a big ugly stud."

Owen unwrapped his sugans and spread his ground tarp out against the rock face where the fire's reflected heat made a comfortable aura. He wrapped himself in his two blankets and settled with back to the wall where he could watch both men. The narrow one sauntered over, grinning down at him.

"Name's North. They call me Ivy. The kid is Missou Holbrook—of Clay County, Missouri. Related to Jesse James, so he says."

"Owen Rutledge."

North's flaxen brows pinched. He squatted down, his lean satyr's face bemused. "Well. Well." He picked up a handful of sand and sifted it between his fingers. "They say you can use a gun. They said it in El Paso. And far north as Cheyenne. They *said* you was a big stud."

Owen nodded and yawned, aware of an aching drowsiness. Such stories were currency across a frontier where men must make their own entertainment, stories passed by mouth during long evening hours in cattle town, mining camp, bunkhouse, and range camp. Tales which lost nothing through many recountings, he thought wryly.

He'd heard of Ivy North too . . . a Rio border gunswift tied into deals of many shades and always shady . . . nothing to pin down. Missou Holbrook was evidently a newcomer—but there was an easy, yet hard-won, competence to the way the boy carried himself. A pity he was siding North . . . Owen sensed that this youth had clean stuff—his righteous, naïve wrath at Abner's presence —but he was traveling in company that would fast bring him to a forking of the road.

Abner returned bearing an armload of dry, crumbling punk which he must have kicked out of a rotten deadfall. He dropped his burden, threw a sizeable chunk on the fire. A flurry of tinder-dust ignited like a hundred fireflies and the flames flared higher.

"Better get out of those wet clothes," Owen advised Abner.

"I never seen such a pair of studs," said North.

The kid Missou stood up, idly lifted his dragoon pistol from holster, spun its fluted cylinder. He glanced around, his gaze stopping on an empty tomato can laying on the bare ground off from the fire. He brought the gun level, took easy and unhurried aim and fired. The can bounded high. It bounced a good dozen feet away. The kid aimed again. A slug sent the can spinning into the outer darkness. Missou had not fired the second shot; his dark, defiant stare swung to Ivy North.

North sheathed his gun, chuckling. "Got to hold your target faster, kid. Suppose that was big stud Rutledge and not a can?"

Owen sleepily closed his eyes. The kid's defiant exhibition became, in North, a cheap bravura. He opened his eyes as Abner jogged his elbow, silently extending dried beef and hardtack from their saddlebags. Owen chewed slowly, washed it down with swallows from his canteen. Afterward he reached for his gunbelt and unholstered the gun. It was a cedar-gripped Navy Colt converted to take metal cartridges. North and Missou watched expectantly, but seeing him proceed to clean it, North smiled thinly and the kid snorted his disgust.

Abner stretched out in his blankets, keeping his eyes open till Owen gave him a nod. He grunted softly, closed his eyes and went to sleep almost at once. Owen smiled faintly. Admittedly their relationship was a strange one, and an inner intuition had warned him not to analyze it too closely. He remembered how once, long after the war and end of slavery, he, with embarrassed roughness, had told Abner to drop the "Mars'." Abner had flashed one of his rare grins and continued with the old address as though nothing had been said. Since Abner had an independent pride of his own, Owen guessed that this was the only token of respect and loyalty that a black man raised in the South could show to a white. On their common quest, Abner recognized him as leader; otherwise, he wore his freedom with the same dignity he had slavery. . . .

Those had been good ones, their youthful days . . . hunting, fishing, swimming, riding, always inseparable.

As far back as memory reached, there had always been Abner, watching over him through boyhood's golden trials with the protective pride of six years' seniority, accepting the white boy's occasionally cruel assumptions of superiority with calm, never obsequious, diffidence. That Abner had been his father's slave was a fact which neither ever forgot . . . then or since. Both had listened to Owen's big, burly father bellow that if that damned monkey Lincoln were elected, war was inevitable.

And so Owen Rutledge at eighteen had marched off with Morgan's gray videttes, bearing on his youthful shoulders the full honor of home and family, the only son. He had soon acquitted himself with a lieutenant's commission, with his shed blood (a slight, romantically unserious wound), but always with honor. It had all been an exercise in honor at first, full of dashing skirmishes, visits home, and parade-ground pageantry.

But Kentucky had been a state divided. The independent and poor-proud peoples of the mountains gave loyalty to the Union; to the Confederacy went the pride of the wealthy slaveowners of the bluegrass plains. Not in Boone's day had Kentucky been a darker or bloodier ground than those four years when a man in the frenzy of battle might unknowingly take the life of father or brother. From this borderline sympathy had grown borderline factions: guerrilla bands who switched loyalties overnight till they degenerated into loyalty to nothing. They donned blue or gray and raided as immediate profit demanded.

One such band had been Cushing Tierney's Raiders. Tierney had begun as the scion of one of Kentucky's finest families, while the sum of his band consisted of inbred hill trash. By 1863 the Confederacy was so scandalized by his repeated turn-coating and attendant massacre, pillaging and rape that Jefferson Davis had officially outlawed him. By early spring of '65 his depredations became so brutal that Morgan's Rifles had been ordered into Tierney's mountain stronghold to run him to ground. Lieutenant Rutledge, now a grimly seasoned veteran, had played a major hand in the bloody battle that had exterminated all but the five raiders, including Cushing Tierney, who escaped and fled down into the bluegrass country.

A month later, Owen Rutledge, weary of war, sickened by defeat of his cause, had returned to his father's isolated farm. He had found house and buildings reduced to cold ashes, fields and meadows a charred and blackened waste. He found mutilated bodies—his father's, his mother's, their slaves. He did not find his two sisters. He found Abner in a thicket where he had crawled with three bullets in him. A spark of life still hung on in the big vital body, and Owen had nourished it carefully.

Later, Abner, sweating from broken fever, had weakly whispered the story. Three days before, five ragged, wild-looking men had come, demanding money of Owen's father. The old man had responded typically. They had shot him and Owen's mother, dragged the screaming girls from the house. They'd rounded up the slaves at rifle point and systematically proceeded to slaughter them. Abner recalled nothing more, except lunging at one of the men, struggling with him for his rifle . . . then the shots. But what of Owen's sisters? "Must've taken 'em both along, Mars' Owen."

Owen left food and water with Abner, then hopelessly picked up a cold trail. It led to the nearest farm, miles away. Only that morning while ditching his fields, the head of the house told him, he had found the two girls' bodies near a spot where some men had evidently camped and gone on. Owen brought the bodies back to the Rutledge farm and interred them with his parents and seven slaves in the family plot.

"I'll stay with you till you're on your feet, Ab," he had told Abner. "Then it's goodbye," to which the big Negro said simply, "Reckon I got to go with you, Mars' Owen."

"The law says I got to pay you now, Ab. There's nothing left."

"I'll ride alongside. Seein's I'm free now, man'll be ridin' where his fancy goes." A shudder had run through him; his voice broke. "My woman Saph is lyin' by your family, Mars' Owen."

That, Owen reflected now, was as much as either had spoken directly then or since of their single-minded mission. At first it had seemed short-lived. Tierney had left a trail of bloody carnage, swinging westward. Then the Federal provost-marshal ordered occupation troops to shoot any of the five outlaws on sight. Two were killed holding up a bank in Lexington. The other three were hunted out of the state. Working west on a thin-clued trail, Owen and Abner found a dead end on the plains of Texas.

The long years that followed ran to pattern. They confined an aimless search to the Southwest, their only reasoned guide being that a man who wished to lose himself would do so on a brawling frontier. They systematically covered a piece of territory, worked when money ran low, drifted to new country, bought drinks for strangers, asked guarded questions, searched a thousand new faces. Crowding strangers who turned out to be the wrong men tempered them to quick danger.

At last the search broke by pure chance. One morning in a little mining town, the name of Yeager Garvey was casually dropped by an old man in a saloon. Owen bought him drinks, plied him with questions. Garvey was prospecting in the hills above the village . . . and now Garvey was dead, leaving them with one slender lead: Blanco Basin.

Owen stared out savagely, unseeingly, at the rain running off the sheltering overhang. Blanco Basin—that was all. Had Cushing Tierney and "Red John" Sykes, his lieutenant, changed their names? Likely enough, for they'd been the big fish; Garvey was a minor member of the gang. Where—and who—might they be now? How much might their appearances have changed in nearly seven years? They might be earning a living as respected merchants or thirty-a-month ranchhands. . . .

"Thinkin', stud?"

Owen looked at North squatting a few feet away, eyes squinted against smoke from the cigarette in his teeth-set grin. "You and the black boy bound for Blanco town? We'll ride in with you."

"Pleasure," Owen said dryly, adding: "We're strangers to the basin."

"Hell, my first time here too . . . looking for a job, by chance?"

Owen shook his head in negation. "You got one here, maybe?"

"Just maybe." North's grin held as he rose and heel-ground his cigarette. "Got to see a man . . . he might have something for you. I'll put in a word if you want."

He tramped across to his bedroll by Missou who was already snoring softly, pulled off his boots and stretched out, sighing out his breath deeply. Owen remained as he was, sitting with chin on knees, his cleaned and loaded gun in his fist beneath his blanket. He stared into the outer darkness, disregarding the dying fire from long habit. A man who stared into fire and then into darkness would be momentarily blinded when his life might depend on clear sight. Despite his marrow-deep exhaustion he sleepily decided to hold wakefulness . . . no telling about Ivy North's stripe. Then within a minute his muscles were lax, his head tilted, and he slept.

THREE

The settlement of Blanco had been one of the northern-most outposts of New Spain, important enough to bring plodding *conductas* up from old Mexico deep into the Sangre de Cristos. Mule trains laden with abundant supplies and rich furnishings for the feudal household of the *hacendados* Rivera, the family whose New World grant from His Catholic Majesty had comprised a good two-thirds of the great Blanco Basin for nearly two centuries.

The last of the Rivera line had been assassinated by one of Armijo's agents during the Mexican War. Ceding of the southwest to the United States had brought only a mild cultural transition to the Blanco Basin; its wealth of rolling grasslands was the key to the continuing prosperity of the American ranchers here. Self-governed almost lawlessly, it was nevertheless so peaceful that officials in the county seat beyond the mountain arm ignored it. Federal, territorial, and county lawmen had no occasion to visit.

Owen Rutledge's knack for storing up scattered fragments of information let him automatically reassess these facts; he bleakly reflected on his need for many more as he and Abner trailed into the main street of Blanco, Ivy North and Missou Holbrook riding ahead. If the basin held the end of his search, he had to bend all he could learn toward that end.

The mid-morning sun picked out stately old adobe and fieldstone buildings whose Andalusian *exótica* contrasted with the interlarding of square, clapboarded frame buildings of a more recent frontier. The night's heavy rain stood in glassy pools along the rut-channeled street, an oozing mire thickly churned by their mounts' hoofs. Ivy North drew rein in front of a dual saloon and store with a one-word legend, CLAIBORNE'S, across its false front.

North wrapped his reins around the tie rail, squinting up at Owen. "Step down. Have one drink on me, anyway."

Owen dismounted. Abner reached down to take his reins. "I'll be a minute, Ab."

"All right, Mars' Owen."

North remarked as they tramped inside with Missou, "Your boy there knows his place for all his sass."

"He's no fool," Owen answered dryly. "Around the border and below we both go in a Mexican cantina . . . but up here colored men have been shot for as much."

The barroom was long, vaulted, and smoke-free this early in the morning. The mahogany bar was innocent of customers. A yeasty tang of beer hung pleasantly in the stale air. Owen ordered a beer; North and Missou took whiskey.

"Here's to sin," North said, tossing off his drink. To the thick-bodied bartender: "I'm North, Ivy North. Claiborne'll be expecting me."

The man paused in the act of mopping at a bar stain. He looked North over carefully, nodded once and in the same motion tilted his head toward a rear door. "Office back there."

"Give my friends another," North said. He tossed a double-eagle on the bar. "Suppose you hold your horses, Rutledge. The man might want to see you . . . might change your mind about working for him."

"Don't bother," Owen murmured.

"No bother." North grinned and sauntered the bar's length to the rear door. He went through it uninvited.

Owen brooded into the schooner, turning it barely tasted between his big hands. He wished Missou weren't here . . . he wanted to ask the bartender a few questions privately. Barmen were always the first to know the most. He shrugged, lifted his glass and drained it. He'd swung from the bar to leave when the office door opened and Ivy North called, "Oh, Rutledge—slow down."

A man stepped out past North and came across the room. A rawboned man who towered above even Owen, his face nearly hidden by a huge beard which spilled like dark hoarfrost over his pleated white shirtfront. His gaunt head with its high, bulging brow had a kind of hungry melancholy in keeping with the conservative black broadcloth he wore like any small merchant. But his skin was deeply sunburned, eye corners meshed with fine wrinkles . . . eyes that were colorless and ceaselessly darting and strangely chill. His age might have been anywhere from thirty-five to fifty-five.

"This here's Matthew Claiborne," North said laconically. "Owen Rutledge."

Claiborne extended a large bony hand, sizing up Owen in a flicking glance. He nodded as if with approval. "Pleasure, sir," he rumbled in a voice soft, yet rich and rolling. Unlike most lofty, loose-jointed men, he was not stooped; he carried himself with an erect military bearing. This, with his name, jolted an echo of recognition in Owen's mind.

"Not General Claiborne? Bloody—"

"Yes, Mr. Rutledge," Claiborne cut in gently. " 'Bloody Matt' Claiborne. My reputation has preceded me, as usual. Will you have a drink with me?"

Owen automatically nodded, held by curiosity. Major-General Matthew Claiborne had been the South's infamous spearhead in the Tennessee border campaigns. Efficient, quick-thinking, always a good officer, never a martinet, he'd yet inspired no love in the troops who had dubbed him "Bloody Matt," this man who'd been willing to coolly sacrifice any number of men to gain or hold a foot of enemy ground. A glory-hunter, they'd called him. . . . Yet, seeing him now, Owen's quick intuition sensed that the man had probably cared nothing for the opinions of his men or his superiors or the Confederacy itself. Claiborne would need to feel himself a power in his own eyes alone, and would have used any cause, any human life, to that end. Now he was uprooted and cast on a strange beach like much other flotsam of the war. Owen guessed that whatever his business here, it would run true to his character.

Claiborne snapped his fingers. "My private bottle, George. Three glasses."

"Four," Ivy North suggested. "Missou Holbrook here's with me."

Claiborne settled his brief, restless glance on young Holbrook. He said with a peculiar flatness, "A kid, Mr. North. A green hand. Besides, you'll be handling this job alone."

Missou met the darting stare levelly, saying, "Even a kid learns by watching, sir."

Claiborne's beard parted in a noiseless laugh. "Why that's the only way, my boy. Set one out for the man-to-be, George."

Owen downed the dark, fiery liquor, let its heat flood through his veins and set down his glass to find Claiborne appraising him. "Mr. Rutledge, I have hold of a large thing here," he announced without preliminary. "I've already gathered some men. Riffraff, a cross-dog outfit. Now I need some special ones . . . of which Mr. North here is the first. I want at least one more."

One crook to another, Owen thought wryly, but Claiborne's unquestioning interpretation of his hard look, seedy tramp's appearance, and generally tough name was a common one. *All right, play it that way awhile; you'll need to learn all you can of the basin situation.* "What's your proposition?"

Claiborne said smilingly, "My business. Unless and until it becomes yours. Suffice it to say I need one man who can lead a few others by the nose. You look like him. How would—"

The sound of a wagon rattling down the street drew Claiborne's attention. He walked quickly to the batwing doors and looked over them. He glanced back and jerked his head at Ivy North who came to stand by him.

"There's Colonel M'Kandless now," Bloody Matt said, and lowered his voice to speak in a rapid whisper. North asked a question or two, listened, nodded. Then he pushed open the swingdoors and stepped onto the porch.

Owen and Missou stepped over beside Claiborne. Looking out above his shoulder, Owen saw a dark-haired girl in her teens being assisted down from a fringe-topped rig by an elderly man. The rig was drawn up before a store downstreet and across from the saloon at a sharp angle.

"That'd be North's job?" he asked casually. "That old man?"

Claiborne's sharp sideglance searched his face with faint suspicion which relaxed with his confiding smile. "That's right. Colonel Amos M'Kandless, owner of Lionclaw—biggest ranch in the basin, and heart of the old Rivera grant."

"North won't take him here . . . broad daylight, the middle of town?"

"The more witnesses, the better. It'll be a fair—" Claiborne chuckled mildly— "a fair fight. I told North to touch that hot-blooded Kentucky pride of the good colo-

nel's. The colonel won't suspect the way of the provoca-
tion, since North is a stranger here. This is an oppor-
tunity we can't let pass—the colonel in town with his
daughter and none of his crew. I hadn't expected it to
come off this easily."

Owen watched the elderly man as he bent to check
one of the team's forehoofs. The colonel moved slowly
and with a severe limp, yet holding himself erect with a
painful and iron pride. He was slight, almost frail-seem-
ing, but his thin features seemed hewn from brown
granite. White mustaches bristled like sabers above a
thin, incisive mouth; deep humor lines saved his face
from cold austerity.

"Like shooting a fish in a rain barrel," Owen said
softly.

"Yes, exactly; the beauty of it." Bloody Matt smiled
thinly.

Owen brushed swiftly past him through the doors just
as Ivy North stepped off the walk and began his catlike
saunter across the street. Behind him, Owen heard the
stunned disbelief in Missou Holbrook's voice: "Mr. Claiborne, you mean to say . . . you sent for him to kill
that crippled old man?"

"What kind of sugar pap were you weaned on, boy?"
Matthew Claiborne said irritably. "You know what North
is, you came in his company."

"Never thought about this," Missou said in a voice
soft and dazed. "Never thought about crowding a crippled old man . . . no fair fight."

"You should have thought of that earlier."

"But that girl—she's in line!"

The boy was teetering on a thin edge of indecision . . .
he was a possible ally, but Owen could not wait. He
stepped down from the walk. Claiborne's voice crackled
behind him: "Stay out of it, Mr. Rutledge. He doesn't
need your help."

"*You* stay out of it," Owen said softly.

"What!"

"The kid was right—it's too heavy a hand to load
against the old man. I'm going to stop it."

Claiborne hauled in a wrathful breath, but before he could speak, Missou Holbrook pulled his dragoon pistol in a fluid movement, cocked it, and rammed it into Claiborne's ribs. "Go ahead, mister." The kid had made his decision; his voice hardened with it. "Stop it."

Owen nodded, pivoted and stepped off the boardwalk, heading after North. He gave Abner a quick shake of his head that said, *This is my affair,* as he passed him.

North had halted a dozen paces from the old man. "Oh, Pappy." He whistled. "You there."

Colonel M'Kandless lowered the horse's hoof, turned with a slow, painful dignity. He said icily, "Did you speak to me, sir?"

"Why you old pone-and-sweet-tater bastard, I meant none other."

Deep crimson mounted to the colonel's face. He brushed back the coat of his white tropical suit with a veined and trembling hand, exposing a belted pistol. His soft drawl thickened. "I am not an unreasonable man. I will hear the meaning of your words, then an apology."

"If you ain't the cockiest old sonuvabitch!"

"Pa," the girl said. It left her as a soft scream. "Pa, don't . . ."

"Cissie, get off out of the way. Hurry."

"North."

Owen had reached street's center, halting in the ankle-deep mud. Then he spoke. North looked at him lazily but did not turn. "Stud, I had just a feeling we might strike sparks. Why I figured on keeping you around. I'll look for'ard to another time. Right now—"

"Right now," Owen said flatly, "you better turn around."

North swung one foot back and made a half-turn, coming motionless with legs braced. His faded eyes were alight, amused. "I'm gonna stomp you, big stud . . . *now!*"

Owen felt the smooth smack of the gun butt against his palm, and as the Navy Colt came level, the whole scene froze in iron clarity. Then the gun blasts merged. Owen brought one foot sideways—a small movement;

North's slug passed between his arm and body. A giant blow wrenched North's head and he fell with his arms and legs splayed from his body. A thin pool of muck splashed with his impact and washed back against his body.

Owen walked to him. He started to bend and saw the back of North's head where his bullet had emerged and straightened. He swallowed against a roiling sickness. A man could get a reputation in all manner of brawls . . . but few bullets killed at once. A man shot in any number of vital spots could live for days. This was his first known killing . . . but North was the real killer and he knew he must hold to that thought and not think of the rest.

He drew an arm across his clammy face and looked at Colonel M'Kandless. The old man faced him stiffly. "I did not ask your help."

"I know you didn't, sir," Owen heard himself say.

"Unfortunately you've placed me in your debt . . ."

"Yes, thank you." Cissie M'Kandless moved close to her father. She was tall, slim in a rangy, colt-lithe way, not pretty; the thin, too-sharp features of her father lay on her face, strained to paleness beneath its Indian-tan. "Thank you from the bottom of my heart. He would have been killed—"

"Cissie," the colonel reprimanded stiffly.

"Oh, you know it's true!" she said passionately.

Owen nodded and touched his hat, then slogged back to the porch, his face iron-hard as he tramped across it to face Claiborne. "Want my answer now?" he asked thinly.

"Why, I have it," Matthew Claiborne said. "You're a purple fool."

"My own, though."

"Well, that may be important to you. But I will advise you to ride on. If you do not, and cross me again in this basin, it will be for the last time."

"Now," Owen said, feeling the backwash of violence grip his body with its trembling reaction, "now you have me shaking."

Missou Holbrook holstered his dragoon as Claiborne gave him a long, measuring look. "You pulled a gun on me, boy. You drift. You could just be shot on sight and no one would care."

Missou's dark eyes moved to the sprawled form of North, and he shook his head slowly, once. Then he slapped open the batwings and went off the porch to his horse. He mounted, reined about and started into a rough canter down the street.

Claiborne took a cheroot from his vest pocket, bit off the end with a savage twist and spat it at Owen's feet. Without a word he turned and walked back to his office.

FOUR

Owen stepped down to the tie rail and untied his bay. "We'll take the horses to the livery stable. I'll put up at the hotel, the livery owner will likely let out his loft to you."

Abner nodded, crossing his hands on his pommel. It was their usual way in a white man's town. "Mars' Owen, that Genril 'Bloody Matt' Claiborne himself?"

Owen swung into his saddle. "The same man. Same kind of man. Got big ideas, warned me to keep out of his way."

"Heard him. Reckon we can handle that, too?"

"No choice as to that now." They kneed their horses down the street toward the big livery barn at its north end. Owen felt an odd pleasure at Missou Holbrook's reaction when the chips were down, confirming his first judgment. Likely he'd not see the kid again, but at least Missou was pointed off from Ivy North's lead.

Meanwhile Owen Rutledge had turned one acquaintance into an enemy to pose an ever-present threat while he remained in the basin. As was his way, Owen had helped Colonel M'Kandless without checking wherefores, and he knew no regret. If he'd made an enemy, he'd also helped a boy and saved an old man's life.

"Please."

They were reining past the mercantile store. Owen glanced absently at the woman standing on the porch as she spoke; then he looked away. "Please," she said again, a little louder, and he realized she'd addressed him.

He ranged over by the porch, touching his hat. "Yes'm?"

"I saw what happened. I'd like to talk to you."

He regarded her wonderingly from the top of her primly coiffed head to the hem of her plain black dress. She was small and in her mid-twenties, with a placid little face rescued from plainness by its pert, tip-tilted nose and vivid blue eyes. A sprinkling of girlish freckles countered its prim, high-chinned poise. Realizing he was staring, Owen said in some embarrassment, "You must be mistaken, ma'am."

"No. You shot a man in front of that saloon."

This laconic directness disconcerted him more; he nodded mutely.

"It's rather private. If you come to my house, I'll tell you my proposal. You may find it a valuable one. . . . I'm Virginia Gilchrist."

Her voice held a twangy New England accent almost alien to his ears, yet with a pleasant crispness. Curiosity alone impelled his slow nod of agreement. "Ab, take the horses on to the stable—"

Abruptly and sharply the girl cut him off. "He is welcome in my house. At least as welcome as you."

Oh Lord, another rabid Abolitionist, Owen thought wearily. Southern-born and bred, he'd met these people rarely, but their attitude left both him and Abner cold. They could not explain a relationship which simply was, which had always been. "If that's your pleasure," he said quietly. "But our horses have to be watered and grained. They've carried us a far way without proper care."

"I see," Miss Gilchrist said primly. "Mister—Ab, my house is the small white one at the very south end of town. When you've finished . . ."

Abner soberly touched the down-furled brim of his ancient slouch hat and took Owen's reins as he stepped down. Owen set off down the boardwalk by the girl, accommodating his long stride to her small, brisk steps. He held a puzzled silence which she did not break.

They turned up the gravel path of a square adobe building on the outskirts, set off from the others. It might have been a Mexican laborer's shanty, now furnished with a heavy coat of whitewash, a white picket fence, and a grassy lawn with geometrically parallel flower beds, all bearing out the personality of an orderly and feminine tenant.

She unlocked the door with a key from her reticule and stepped in, holding the door for him. He jerked off his hat and ducked his head beneath the low jamb. She nodded him to a sagging, battered divan with a faded-rose pattern on which he gingerly settled his bulk, knees drawn uncomfortably high.

"In Boston I would serve tea at this time of day," she observed with the faintest smile. "But you've come a distance, and in this country . . . coffee?"

"Yes'm, please."

She disappeared through a rear doorway, and he gave the small front room a careful attention. The worn rug and few pieces of furniture was spared shabbiness by precise, balanced placement and spotless cleanliness. A shelf on the wall held a number of fragile crystal pieces . . . dishes and figurines. Her only display heirlooms, he supposed. With a sudden poignancy he remembered his mother's pride, the tasteful parlor where she had entertained. . . .

Virginia Gilchrist returned bearing a tray with a small coffeepot which she set on a taboret facing the divan. She filled two china cups. "No cream, I'm afraid. Sugar, Mr.—?"

"Rutledge, Owen Rutledge. No thank you."

He lifted the steaming brew, sipped it as she drew up a straight-backed cane-bottomed chair, sat, and folded her hands on her lap. "Now, Mr. Rutledge, to business. . . . You're a stranger here, but have you heard of the Rivera family?"

"Clan of Spaniards that used to hold this basin on a king's grant, yes, ma'am."

She cocked her head slightly, vivid eyes measuring him coolly. "You haven't heard, probably, that the original charter granted by the Spanish Crown to Don Felipe Rivera is—was in my possession?"

"News to me."

"As it was to me when I learned of it nine months ago on my father's death. We were quite poor; his will bequeathed me little more than his strongbox holding a few papers, mostly of indebtedness, and a sealed envelope containing the charter and a letter of explanation. It seems that I, as my father's only child, am the legal heiress to all the property stipulated in the old grant."

Owen caught himself leaning forward with interest and now he straightened casually, his words tinged with a shade of doubt: "Your father was a poor man . . . and you hadn't heard of this before?"

She stiffened a little. "He was, and I had not. But the story, as related in his letter, explained a strange situation."

In 1792, she went on, her great-grandfather, a Boston merchant named Samuel Gilchrist, had been supercargo of a ship with goods consigned for Monterey. There his native and cultured charm had ingratiated him with *Californio* high society . . . with the grandees Rivera, who had come from the eastward territory to visit relatives. He later married the current family-head's only daughter and returned with her to Boston. After the Mexican War and transferral of southwestern properties to the United States, the disentangling of numerous documents resulted in the dispatch of the original Spanish charter for Blanco Basin to Samuel Gilchrist's eldest son. But John Gilchrist was a cautious, well-to-do merchant with no desire to risk money in a long-drawn legal battle with other claimants; the question of southwestern property right was still vague and unsettled. The charter was passed to his son, Virginia's father, a frail invalid under whose hand the family business had decayed. His only remaining possession of value was an ancient document which might prove the key to fortune—but it lay useless in his sick, timid, poverty-stricken hands.

" 'I did not have the courage or the means to use it,' " Virginia softly quoted her father's letter. " 'You have the courage, daughter, and the wit and the will, and you may find a way.' So I sold our house, Mr. Rutledge, and came out here to see . . . if there was a way."

Owen was silent a moment, scowling into his empty cup. Doubt still shaded his voice: "You mentioned that you *had* it."

"The charter was stolen from me only yesterday."

"How?"

"I had it wrapped in an oilcloth and locked in my trunk, stored beneath a cupboard in the kitchen. Someone stole in while I was at work, forced the lock, and took only the document."

"You tell anyone where it was?"

"No. . . ." She sounded doubtful, then added emphatically, "No."

So somebody knew and she's not saying, Owen thought sardonically, and went on: "Then who do you think stole it?"

"Colonel Amos M'Kandless," she said unhesitatingly, and then, quickly: "Yes, you saved his life . . . he must have appeared the very soul of the Southern gentleman. So he may be, but not where his property is concerned. . . . Lionclaw, his ranch, is the heart of the old Rivera grant. When I learned of this on my arrival at Blanco, I went to see him. He greeted me courteously and heard my story. He mocked it politely at first, but when I was insistent he grew angry—said I was a cheap fraud trying to perpetrate a large-scale swindle."

"You show him the charter?"

"Of course. He pronounced it a clever forgery after

barely glancing at it . . . and my story, a fantastic hoax."

"A strange story, you'll own," Owen observed dryly.

"I told you it was," she said tartly. "Well, what could I do? I had enough money to buy this house, then learned that the local schoolhouse needed a teacher. So I have a job and very meager salary . . . hardly enough to contest a claim against the wealthy colonel. I have no ties back East. I could only stay on, hoping for . . ." she shrugged, looking down at her folded hands . . . "a miracle."

Owen frowned. Told in her direct and cool manner, the story had a ring of truth. If she was a fraud, she was an incredibly convincing one, who seemed what she appeared—a transplanted Boston schoolmistress. He stirred his feet uncomfortably. "This is interesting, ma'am. Very. But . . ."

"I want your services for a very simple reason. You're a stranger with no visible interest here. You saved a helpless old man by shooting an attempted assassin. That showed both competence and integrity. Our talk has also borne out your . . . moderate good breeding."

"Thank you. And you want me to rectify my mistake and shoot Colonel M'Kandless?" He immediately regretted his perverse response.

She said steadily and with no heat, "I do not. I want you to find the charter and return it to me. With its transferral to my family a matter of government record, it's useless to anyone but me, but plainly dangerous to anyone with an opposing claim."

"Are you certain," Owen said very slowly, "that nobody but Colonel M'Kandless has such a claim?"

She hesitated. "There is another—Matthew Claiborne. He came to the basin a month ago, ostensibly to buy a saloon, actually to force a claim of his own. Somehow he'd come into possession of a thirty-five-year-old Mexican grant laying claim to all the old Rivera land. It's made out, so I've heard, to one General Estevan Torres, evidently a reward for loyal service . . . and signed by Armijo, the last Mexican governor of New Mexico, I believe."

"A genuine claim?"

"I haven't seen the paper. I understand that Claiborne showed it to Colonel M'Kandless and they had hot words . . . the upshot being that the colonel threatened to shoot Claiborne on sight. Since then Claiborne has quietly hired several shiftless toughs. He doesn't have nearly enough money to fight his claim against the colonel's in court either; doubtless he intends to force him off Lionclaw and afterward deal from a more equal position."

"He tried to get M'Kandless killed today," Owen pointed out.

"That would be surer still. He would then have to deal with only the colonel's brother and the daughter, Cissie. I doubt if the colonel has any other heirs. The brother, I have heard, is not of the colonel's fiber, and Cissie is little more than a child. Probably he could bully and frighten them into giving him at least a large chunk of Lionclaw without difficulty."

"I've met Matthew Claiborne," Owen said, "and I'd put him down as the more likely to steal your charter—to remove another claimant."

"But only M'Kandless . . ." Again he noted her uncertain pause. . . . "Only M'Kandless knew of the charter; I spoke to him in private."

"If he did take it, he had no reason not to destroy it."

"I've thought of that. Still he might keep it if only till he ascertained its authenticity. I'm assuming that his righteous designation of me as a fraud was a fraud of his own. Actually he must have been alarmed. Such Spanish grants have been often given precedence in American courts, and—after all, what becomes of a gentleman who loses his estate?"

"You tell me."

She leaned forward earnestly. "Mr. Rutledge, you have given me some discourteous replies, and I understand your feelings. . . . You are—a tramp proficient with a gun. Isn't that it, bluntly? And you resent a woman who would ordinarily snub you on the street now stooping to ask your help when she needs it. You are right, of course, so let me put the proposition on a purely business basis. If you will investigate the theft of my charter, I'll pay you well. In my present occupation, I may be long accumulating the money. If you leave the basin before then, I will forward the money to whatever address you leave."

"This charter," he said thoughtfully. "A kind of life-line for you, isn't it, though you can't use it?"

"You need not consider that," she said stiffly. "How much do you want? I'll put it in writing."

"Fifty dollars, and that won't be necessary," he said roughly.

Her face cleared. "Why, that's more than reasonable."

He shrugged. "You're trusting me—and that's unreasonable. I might sell the charter for a lot more to either Claiborne or M'Kandless."

"I don't believe you would do that, Mr. Rutledge."

He smiled faintly. "Where do I begin?"

"You helped Colonel M'Kandless. In return he should be glad to give you employment. You're a resourceful man; you'll think of something. If you become convinced that he doesn't have the charter, I will forfeit the fifty dollars."

Owen stroked his chin absently. "How many men on the Lionclaw crew?"

"Oh . . . I should say twenty, not counting the Mexican tenants whom the colonel inherited when he bought the place. It's a thriving affair."

Why not? Owen thought. A man might help himself and this girl too. He would have to reconnoiter all of Blanco Basin to find his men, and Lionclaw's twenty-man crew was as good a place as any to begin.

"I'll do my best."

"Thank you." A warm wave of relief colored her face. She followed him to the door. Someone rapped at it briskly.

"That should be your friend," Virginia observed, opening it. ". . . . Oh, Charlie."

The young man who stood on the threshold smiled casually. "I didn't know you had company, Ginny."

"Mr. Rutledge, this is Charles McVey—Blanco's only lawyer. This is Owen Rutledge, Charlie."

McVey extended a firm hand. He was of medium height, about of an age with Owen, cutting a slim and elegant figure in his inexpensive black suit. His light blond hair was close-cropped above an oval cherub's face of fresh, ruddy color. Owen thought that McVey's most valuable asset as a lawyer must be his eyes—a wide, innocuous blue.

"You're new to the basin, sir," McVey said, as pleasantly as though encountering a big, rough-looking tramp in Virginia Gilchrist's parlor were an everyday matter. Owen said yes, as he shook hands.

"I don't want to intrude, Ginny. . . ."

"I was leaving." Owen clamped on his hat. "Day, ma'am, Mr. McVey."

"Goodbye, Mr. Rutledge," she said warmly, "and thank you."

That must be her beau, Owen thought as he tramped down the gravel path. An unbidden consideration struck him: was McVey the unmentioned party whom she'd told of the trunk-stored charter? Unusual for him, Owen could not make a quick judgment about the young lawyer: McVey had a perfectly-cultivated attorney's blandness which closeted his thoughts from the sharpest eye. It was a thing to keep in mind.

Turning onto the street, he saw Abner come from a store carrying a bulging flour sack, and went to meet him.

"Bought some noon grub, Mars' Owen. We kin walk out from town an' build us a cook fire."

They went down to the riverbank and Abner gathered brush while Owen scraped a hollow for the fire and told of the bargain with Virginia Gilchrist. "I think she rings true, Ab. We can find out what she wants to know and maybe what we want to know, same time."

Abner's dark face creased approvingly. "I liked the cut of that little lady, Mars' Owen. Lowdown 'bolition foolery an' all."

FIVE

Colonel Amos M'Kandless had made the ancient house of Rivera his own home. The main building was a huge block of whitewashed adobe, two stories high and set on a fieldstone foundation. The front veranda columns supported an iron-railinged gallery which ran around all four sides. Two new one-storied flanking wings were of hand-hewn pine timbers, green and still oozing pitch. A park of towering cottonwoods surrounded and shaded the house and its outbuildings, set well off from the main structure.

Owen and Abner caught their first sight of it at late afternoon, topping a rise nine miles east of Blanco town. The long slope rolled into the grassy flats where Lionclaw headquarters lay. "That's near big an' fine as any bluegrass plantation," Abner observed.

Owen nodded absently as he gigged his bay down the slope. It was a fine and peaceful old land, this basin, with a long-established, aristocratic Spanish culture which men like Colonel M'Kandless, himself of old Kentucky's finest, would have preserved and enhanced. Now another breed of man, a violent breed, like Ivy North and Matthew Claiborne *and Owen Rutledge,* he thought with wry honesty, were ready to disrupt it into bloody warfare for their own ends. His hired killer's failure to kill M'Kandless would hardly deter Claiborne. He would only change his mode of offense, and no telling how it would come.

They rode past a row of Mexican shanties where coffee-brown women and children stared curiously at Owen's companion, of a color far darker than theirs. Finally they turned up a gravel buggy drive which curved gracefully athwart the front of the big house.

At their approach three people on the wide veranda broke off conversation. Owen reined in his fiddlefooting bay by the steps, and touched his hat to Cissie M'Kandless who was sitting on the top step, slapping a riding crop against her palm. She wore a gray riding habit and was bareheaded. She smiled warm recognition and respectfully said nothing, waiting for her father to speak.

The colonel, a cool, distinguished figure in white flannels and a Panama hat, sat in a rocking chair, a glass of brandy in his hand. By him stood a tall, middle-aged man in worn range clothes whose leathery face, seamed with fine-grained lines, outshaded his pale brown eyes, eyes which laid a neutral, watchful gaze on Owen.

The colonel painfully uncrossed his legs and slowly rose. He stumbled as he took a short step forward. The tall man instinctively reached a hand, as quickly drew it back unnoticed when the proud old man recovered balance, limped slowly to the veranda edge. He nodded stiffly. "Good afternoon, sir. Will you step down?"

Owen swung to the ground and turned, lifting a foot to the bottom step. M'Kandless' courteous poise relaxed with his curious scrutiny of Owen's face. "There is something very familiar about you; I marked it this morning in town. What is your name?"

Owen told him.

"Rutledge, of course!" A warm smile broke the colonel's polite austerity; he held out a wasted and trembling hand which Owen took. "Young Owen . . . Harry Rutledge's boy. I served with your father in the Kentucky legislature, just before the war. He often spoke of his only son . . . a law student."

Owen smiled too. "You're *Senator* M'Kandless, sir? Your surname is one of Kentucky's oldest, of course . . . but we never met."

"I am proud to shake hands with Harry Rutledge's son before I die. And how is your father?"

"Dead, sir. The war," Owen said shortly.

"I'm genuinely sorry to hear it," the colonel said quietly. "He was a fine man . . . too forceful and outspoken—I should say too honest—to have lasted long in politics. During his brief tenure in the Senate, I came to respect him highly."

Owen smiled. "That was Pa."

"I've gotten out of touch," the colonel went on. "Rather than remain to watch the downfall of the Confederacy, my family and I came to New Mexico and this peaceful basin late in '64. Afterward we severed all ties in Kentucky. Too many painful memories."

"A good many Kentuckians can say as much, sir," Owen said quietly.

"Yes." The colonel's hawk eyes were intent. "You will forgive my seeming ingratitude of this morning, I hope? I had forgotten that a gentleman's honor must express itself in different ways in a different land. You gave that fellow his chance . . . and saved a sick and aging man." His mustaches twitched with his smile. "A fact I don't mind confessing to the son of Rutledge."

Owen knew a quick stab of shame, thinking of his purpose here—which he must conceal. "I will have to confess, sir, that I am here to ask for a job. Abner and I have worked cows."

"Abner?" The same bodyservant you had as a boy? Your father used to speak of him, too. . . . Of course there's a place for him on my crew. But I can offer you better, Owen. I have need of a man . . ." He coughed embarrassedly . . . "A sort of general secretary. I'm no hand at figures, and the ranch books are in a sorry state. Also, of late, certain questions have arisen about my legal ownership of this ranch and I need a legal advisor, one I can trust. You've studied law. . . ."

"Thank you, sir."

The colonel smiled broadly. "It's settled, then. Here, shake hands with my segundo, Paul Dirksen. Paul, show Abner to the bunkhouse—"

"If you don't mind," Owen interrupted, "I'll see him there."

"I understand," the colonel nodded wisely. "But there are Mexicans, a Ute wrangler, and two mulattoes on my crew. They work in team with the whites; there is no discord."

"Nevertheless I'd like to see the bunkhouse, Colonel."

The colonel laughed. "Your protective loyalty to your man is admirable, Owen. Very well . . . and look over the place, if you like. Be back at the house in time to clean up. We eat at six sharp."

Cissie got quickly to her feet and came down the steps. "I—I'd like to thank you again, Mr. Rutledge. For this morning."

She colored deeply as he spoke, and Owen realized her extreme shyness. She must be seventeen or eighteen, an age when Southern-bred belles were long-groomed to crinoline and cotillions. But she was a plain girl on a lonely ranch with a stern father, a combination which would have easily formed her withdrawn and tomboy manner. Her riding habit was well-worn and dusty, her nut-brown hair carelessly caught in a loose knot at the back of her neck. But her eyes were a light clear hazel that made him think of a poet's line about windows of the soul.

He removed his hat with careful courtesy, saying gently, "Glad I was there, Miss Cissie."

She blushed more furiously, and ducked her head. Owen smiled and picked up his mount's trailing reins. Abner stepped down, and he and Owen followed Paul Dirksen to the corral, leading their horses. Walking apace of Dirksen, Owen was aware of the man's sharp, shrewd sideglance, and he thought, *It'll come now, all the questions*. But Dirksen said only, in a deep musical drawl, "So the kunnel knew your pappy?" and Owen nodded, and that was all.

They turned their horses into the corral and carried their saddles to the harness shed. As Owen went inside close behind Abner, he said softly, "If we find one of our men in the bunkhouse and there's trouble . . . we don't start it, Ab. Not here."

"I know, Mars' Owen."

Owen's conscience was already smarting from this necessary subterfuge; he didn't intend to violate the colonel's generous confidence further with violence. They'd waited nearly seven years . . . could wait a while longer.

His real purpose in accompanying Abner to the bunk-house was to learn whether Tierney or Sykes were on the crew. There was a chance that either might recognize Abner, whose thick powerful body and strong-graven face were not easily forgotten; if so, there'd be immediate trouble. Only Abner could identify the pair positively; Owen had seen Cushing Tierney but once, briefly and at a distance, when Morgan's Rifles had crushed the guerrilla band. He remembered a wolf-gaunt form and a fierce, pinched face, nothing more.

Some of the crew were lined up at the wash bench in front of the low log building, waiting their turn to wash up for supper. Abner's passive stare fixed the face of each as they passed, and then they went through the doorway into the puncheon-floored room. Several men were resting on their bunks. Owen met the feisty stare of a thin, short man who was removing his brush chaps. His bushy black hair bristled over a thin and predatory face. He came at once to his feet, a man who evidently compensated for his lack of size with a bantam-cock strut and a fiercely assertive manner.

"What're you staring at, bucko?"

"Nothing," Owen said mildly, idly shifting his glance around the bare interior of the bunkroom. The man's flat challenge, this time to Abner, brought his eyes quickly back.

"Black boy, you see something interesting over here?"

"Simmer down, Fitz," Dirksen said. "The Negro's a new hand, and Rutledge here is a friend of the kunnel's." He added apologetically to Owen, "Fitz is always this way with newcomers, don't mind him any."

Fitz glowered and sank back on his bunk. At once his banjo eyes shuttled back to Abner. "Black boy, you keep starin' me over. I lived too long in Tennessee to take that off a—"

"You talk a lot," Owen said, and was sorry then. It was all Fitz had needed. He mouthed a soft, foul epithet as he lunged to his feet, spreading his wiry arms. *He's the kind wants to jump every big man he sees, and now he's got the excuse,* Owen thought. He glanced at

Dirksen, but the segundo said nothing, only looked on with that neutral, quiet gaze. In a few words, it had developed to a personal antagonism in which no seasoned frontiersman would interfere.

Owen felt a helpless, half-amused irritation as Fitz began circling him. *Should I step on him,* he wondered, *or just blow him over?* The faintest grin touched his lips and Fitz saw it and rushed in, face twisted with fury. His arms windmilled wildly. Owen cuffed them aside, grabbed him by the scruff of the neck and sent him stumbling away. Fitz pivoted back and bored in. A wild swing caught Owen on the nose. In the blaze of pain, he forgot restraint. He fisted his hand in the little man's shirtfront and carried him back to slam him hard against an upper bunk. Fitz was lifted off the floor, legs flailing wildly; the sideboard caught him across the shoulders with a crash that snapped his head back. He gave an agonized yell. Owen's anger cleared at once and he released Fitz, who fell to the floor and lay rubbing his back, eyes blazing up undiluted hatred at Owen.

"You took a grizzly by the tail, Fitz," Dirksen observed with no sympathy, and to Owen with mild reproof: "Man your size can't afford to lose his temper, Rutledge."

"No," Owen agreed.

His sharp old eyes twinkling, the colonel reached the bottle of Madeira across the table to refill Owen's glass. He chuckled. "Quite a man, your father. I'll never forget the time when he announced before the entire State Senate that first seeing Abe Lincoln's picture had converted him to that Darwin fellow's new-fangled theory of evolution. Kentuckian sentiment divided as it was, his remark almost broke up the assembled distinguished gentlemen into fisticuffs."

Owen smiled perfunctorily. In him mounted an uneasiness compounded of impatience and quandary. There was a thing that had to be said, and he did not know how to break it. He let his gaze travel the dining room, taking in the two fine paintings and the tasteful antiques

—undoubted legacy of the M'Kandless ancestral home. The table was spread with white linen and gleaming silverware, centered by two hand-wrought candelabras. It stirred him nostalgically . . . casual refinement, gracious living, fine wine, good after-dinner conversation. It was as much a part of his past as of the colonel's. It would have been tempting to accept the offered position and forget the old mission. But a man could not live in the past; these things no longer belonged to his world.

He raised his glass and across its rim caught Cissie's eye. She sat opposite, wearing a bright frock, and the candlelight caught softly on her hair, now braided and wrapped in a shining corona around her head. He smiled and her freshly scrubbed face blushed quickly. She made a pleasant and healthy picture, and he wished fleetingly that he was ten years younger, a lifetime younger in experience. He sipped his wine and set the glass down to catch the colonel's measuring look.

"You have your father's size," M'Kandless observed. "Almost his spit'n' image . . . except your quiet manner. That's your mother's part, of course. I met her once, a most charming woman. Is she still living, perhaps?"

"No. The war didn't spare—"

"Can't we discuss something else?" the colonel's brother asked pettishly.

Owen's first thought on meeting Reed M'Kandless was that the family blood had run thin in the younger brother. Reed was only in his forties, but indoor confinement and lack of exercise had slackened and slumped his body and inclined him to stoutness. His dark hair was thinning, his precisely-clipped spade beard gray-shot. His face did not show the mottled floridness of an inveterate drinker, but his milky eyes were deeply pouched in the soft paleness of his cheeks. He had been introduced as handling most ranch affairs since the colonel had been thrown from a mettlesome bronc several years ago and his right leg permanently stiffened. But Owen had guessed that this was courtesy title to cover a shiftless and parasitical relative.

"War, I believe, is hardest on the women who wait for its end," the colonel observed soberly, misinterpreting Owen's broken statement. He added with a dry smile, "Reed is sensitive on subjects of violence," and switched the subject.

Owen toyed with his wine glass, only half-listening. Leaving the bunkhouse, he'd caught Abner's brief, negative shake of head to indicate that neither man they sought was on the Lionclaw crew. That finished Owen's own business, leaving only Virginia Gilchrist's.

From the moment of the colonel's cordial recognition of him, Owen had known increasing doubt that Amos M'Kandless had contrived to steal the Rivera charter. The half-hour of conversation they had shared during the meal had hardened doubt to conviction. Virginia had believed that he'd feigned his accusation of her, yet Owen knew there was not a shred of deceit in this old man's withered frame.

It was not a thing which Virginia Gilchrist, reared in a merchant family and used to sharp business practices, would easily understand. It was called honor, and it was the backbone of a life dead, war-shattered. An old-fashioned, antebellum, perhaps foolishly unrealistic integrity of character, but it had been the Southern aristocracy's greatness, of which this ailing, silver-maned lion of a man was a . . . relic? . . . rather a living testimonial. Owen Rutledge was the only deceiver here, and his impulsive pride impelled him to the truth.

"Colonel," he said slowly, "I met a young woman today. You know her . . . Virginia Gilchrist."

The colonel lifted his napkin, patted his lips. "Yes, Owen?"

"She said that she had shown you a document . . . a Spanish charter that fell into her family's possession after the Mexican War."

"That is true." The old man's tone had gained a testy edge.

Owen drew a deep breath, knowing he could still dissemble and keep this man's liking, knowing, too, that he would not. "Yesterday this charter was stolen from her house. She believes that you high-graded it."

"You believed her?"

Owen didn't answer directly. "I agreed to come here, ask you for a job, try to find out if the charter was in your possession. Believe me, sir, I did not intend to play on your friendship with my father to gain your confidences; then, I didn't know who you were."

The colonel crumpled his napkin and threw it in his plate. He stood hastily, knocked over his chair, stumbled and grasped at the table for support. Then he turned and slowly limped to a window, hands clasped behind his back. His slight frame was stiff with anger, his voice shaking slightly:

"Will you leave, sir?"

Owen let out a breath of resignation. "As you wish, Colonel."

"Pa!" Cissie's exclamation was shocked and objecting.

"You heard, daughter. This man is an errand-boy for that cheap woman . . . that lying fraud."

"That isn't fair," Cissie said exasperatedly. "If she tried to dupe you, she did no less to Mr. Rutledge. He's not to blame!"

"He came into my house, ate at my board, took advantage of my hospitality," the colonel said brittlely, "all under a deceitful guise."

"Pa, this isn't the bluegrass!"

"Changed circumstances do not soften the spine of a gentleman. You're young; you'll learn that many a blackguard wears a white fleece." The colonel swung a blue lightning gaze on Owen. "What was your price? Thirty pieces of silver?"

Owen felt his own hot flush. He knew how tawdry the answer would sound, knew the old man would take any explanation as evasive. He said quietly, "Fifty dollars."

"Your father would kill you with his own hands," the colonel said harshly.

Cissie looked speechlessly at her father, then at Owen; he gave her a slight, almost imperceptible shake of head. He rose, reached for his hat on the rack of staghorns by the door, and tramped around the table, heading for the parlor's connecting archway. Passing Reed M'Kandless, he glimpsed a faint, malignant pleasure in the man's face, and was puzzled, and then forgot it as he went through the parlor. He halted by the front door as Cissie's quick steps came up behind him, turned to face her.

"I . . . I feel so ashamed, Mr. Rutledge."

"You needn't, Miss Cissie. Not on my account, and surely not for your father."

"I—I don't. I understand him. And you, too." She laughed, shakily and in some confusion. "Why is life so puzzling? You must have been eighteen once."

"Believe it or not," he smiled.

"Oh you." She ducked her hotly blushing face and toed smilingly at the carpet. Then, soberly: "I hope you won't go too far. Pa won't listen now of course. But later he'll remember that you saved his life, that you told him why you came openly and of your own will. If he doesn't, I'll remind him."

"I wouldn't," Owen said quickly. "I have no reason to stay—now. Best to let the matter die."

She shook her head sadly. "I guess I still don't understand, not really. This foolish, foolish thing—honor. It's narrow, intolerant. And it's a man's thing, I believe, though perhaps," she added with sharp bitterness, "a woman would understand."

"You are a woman, Miss Cissie," Owen said gently. *A warm-hearted and gentle one and some man will be a lucky one,* he added silently. "You're right about honor. A man's thing. We have to live by it—to a woman's heartbreak, I suppose, but . . ." He shrugged, opened the door.

"I hope," Cissie M'Kandless said softly, "you find whatever it is you're trying to find, Mr. Rutledge. . . . Goodbye."

He headed for the bunkhouse, feeling a strong relief as he breathed deeply in the cool twilight. *Well, that's done.* With his regret at this harsh period to a brief friendship was mingled a curiosity about Reed M'Kandless . . . the sly, fleeting satisfaction that man had shown as he left. *You're getting too damned suspicious,* Owen thought. *His name is Reed M'Kandless, he's the colonel's brother, no mistaking that.* No doubt Reed was pleased that there would after all be no addition to the household, showing up Reed's sloth by his industry.

Reaching the bunkhouse, Owen fumbled for the latch, swung the door wide. He blinked against the smoke-hazed lamplight. The crew was sprawled in bunks, mending harness, reading, or talking. Activity broke off as he stepped over the threshold. He caught Abner's eye, tilted his head slightly backward, and Abner immediately swung off his bunk and came over.

"Get your stuff," Owen murmured. "We're leaving."

Abner nodded, his stolid face unchanging, and tramped back to his bunk. He pulled his warbag from beneath it and began rolling up his sugans. Paul Dirksen came lazily to his feet and sauntered to Owen.

"Leavin'?" There was puzzled curiosity in his drawl. Owen nodded.

Dirksen put out a calloused hand and Owen took it. "Sort of pleased when you hired on. Thought, 'Now the kunnel'll have a man to look after his interests, not—' " The segundo broke off, stoically. *Not his brother,* Owen knew he'd begun to say. "Sorry. Anything I can do?"

Owen shook his head. "Thanks. And so long."

Owen's gear was still packed on his saddle, and in the harness shed he waited as Abner fastened on his own, quietly telling the Negro what had happened. "Then what we do now, Mars' Owen?" Abner asked as they trudged toward the corral, lugging their hulls.

"We go back to town," Owen said grimly. "We tell Miss Gilchrist what I learned. Then we start looking. You're going to take a sight at the face of every man jack in this basin if we have to start a small war in the doing."

SIX

Virginia sat on the cane-bottomed chair, her back straight, her small face placid and composed in the lamplight, bent above her work. At her feet was a crocheting bag full of afghan squares, and her fingers plied a needle with quick deftness, stitching these together. Charles McVey shifted his weight restlessly on the sagging divan, frowning faintly.

"You're quiet this evening, Ginny."

She looked up with a preoccupied smile. "Am I, Charlie?"

"Thinking about the big fellow . . . Rutledge?"

Her hands stilled on the material. "As a matter of fact, yes. I might have sent him into . . . anything."

He smiled. "We barely said hello, but I should say that there is a man who was weaned to hard fortune long ago. He'll take care of himself. He'll find your charter too, if M'Kandless has it."

Her fingers moved quickly again. "Don't you think he has it, Charlie?"

"I wouldn't say, Virginia," McVey said in a careful, neutral tone. "A lawyer's caution, you know."

After a moment's long silence, he said almost irritably, "You wouldn't have toyed with the thought that . . . perhaps that I . . . would you?"

Her gaze was very direct, and McVey flinched beneath his bland composure. "If I had thought so, Charlie, you would have heard so."

"Yes, of course," he murmured awkwardly. "But I was the only one you told of the charter's location . . . in your trunk. Naturally, if first suspicion is to be fixed—"

She smiled slowly. "Stop being the attorney. I told

you because I trusted you. I had to talk matters over with *someone,* and you were logical . . . a legal mind, as well as my only friend here. The person who stole the charter simply searched for it and found it."

"I imagine," he nodded, with no trace of the cynical disavowment he felt. When Virginia Gilchrist had first come to the basin, they had naturally gravitated together . . . two young people of similar interests—mostly business, law, and literature. Yet, where Virginia's inclinations were natural to one of her temperament and background, McVey, a poor farmer's son, had deliberately acquired a cultured veneer toward the furthering of his career. He was looking for a wife who would keep step with such a man.

But Virginia was full of her own ambition, otherwise cold to everything except her own genteel and insular existence. He could always look elsewhere; that bothered him less than his smarting ego. Women had always been easy marks for his bland charm . . . this plain little schoolteacher was not. Meanwhile, he thought with secret satisfaction, their brief friendship had already proved unexpectedly profitable. He must not break off his evening and week-end afternoon visits with her too quickly; it might arouse the suspicion that now, to his relief, she did not feel.

Watching her through half-lidded eyes, he wondered whether a man might someday break her composed restraint and find warmth beneath. He'd never really tried —always keeping their relations on the basis of the dispassionate personal friendship she'd established.

He rose now casually, circled behind her chair and stood a moment. She did not look up. He set his hands lightly on her shoulders. "Ginny—"

She gave a little twist and his hands fell away; she was stiffly motionless then, not looking at him. "Charlie," she said brittlely, "it's getting late."

Her response sparked his prideful temper. "Virginia, you can't lock yourself up forever. You're certainly intelligent and perceptive enough to know I haven't been

coming here these weeks only for *talk*! I'd hoped . . .
never mind. Someday you may be sorry."

"Perhaps," she said inflexibly. "But you may be even
sorrier in a moment, Charlie."

The inference was plain. He said with distinct dignity:
"Very well, Virginia. Good night."

"Good night."

She did not accompany him to the door, and he closed
it with just enough violence, and headed down the gravel
path. He halted beneath a spreading cottonwood whose
moon-caught branches struck black shadow-patterns
about him, pausing to pull out a cigar. He drew it alight
with a savage breath, thinking blackly, *Damned cold
little frump. As if I need her!* His temper cooled quickly
to a darkness-hidden smile. Hell, that was as good a way
as any to break it off . . . and save more evenings of talking about dead authors over tea. Besides, there was her
precious charter . . . if it was valuable. He'd meant to
check on that, and now was a good time.

He strode downstreet with long impatient strides to the
darkened business building where he had his office. He
loped up the rickety stairs and down a corridor. He
fumbled out his keys, let himself into his office, groped
for the lamp and lighted it. The sallow light spread to the
dingy corners of the little cubbyhole and he gave it a
single circling glance of distaste; in this peaceful valley,
shallow premium was placed on a lawyer's services. He
unlocked a drawer of his rolltop desk, drew out a manila
folder and removed from it an oilcloth-wrapped packet.

His cherubic features sharpened eagerly as he removed
the wrapping and with infinite care spread out the
browned and fragile document on his desk, his fingers
trembling. The charter was penned in the delicate hand of
a court secretary, the ink faded to near-illegibility; at the
bottom was the Spanish monarch's bold signature, and
beneath this the wax seal of the royal arms. The key to a
fortune . . . if he handled his cards right. Years shaved
off his goal of the state bench by a little judiciously applied semi-blackmail.

Matthew Claiborne, he had long decided, was the

man to watch in the forthcoming crisis between his and Colonel M'Kandless' land claims. Claiborne was shrewd and absolutely unscrupulous; in his hands would rest the future of Lionclaw ranch and Blanco Basin. M'Kandless, old and ailing, could not long hold the prize of Lionclaw's great acres. When Claiborne had the ranch and believed himself securely in possession—that was the time to present him with evidence of an older and more substantial claim that his own Mexican grant. McVey knew ways to make Claiborne pay through the nose for the document without danger to himself—on the threat of returning it to Virginia Gilchrist, in whose hands it might someday wreck Claiborne's whole victory.

McVey carefully rewrapped the parchment and slipped it into his coat pocket. As a hesitant afterthought, thinking of the dark road ahead, he drew a nickel-plated, double-barreled pocket pistol from the open desk drawer, dropped it in his pocket. He blew out the lamp, locked his office and left hurriedly for the livery stable. He ordered the hostler to saddle his short-coupled billy horse. Five minutes later he was riding south from town on a moon-flooded dirt road which wended along the riverbank.

Ahead presently he saw a sprinkling of oily lights which was Mextown, a shallow cluster of adobe shacks situated in the riverbottom. A cur picked him up and yapped furiously at the heels of his mount till he cursed it off. He rode down the narrow dirt street, irritably aware of the faces appearing at doors and windows to speculate on the night appearance here of a lone *gringo*. But they had seen him before and they watched with only sleepy and half-hostile interest as he dismounted before the Ortega adobe.

McVey threw reins and stepped to the low door, raising his knuckles. Before he could knock, the door was quickly opened, and, "Come in, Carlos," Abrana Ortega said, her voice hushed and breathless.

He stepped inside without removing his hat, giving the chili-hung walls, the small plaster shrine and hand-fashioned furniture, his sardonic glance. The girl closed the door and turned swiftly to face him, her dark full skirt swirling out from dainty tanned ankles. "This is the first time in a week, Carlos . . . still the pale *Yanqui* creature takes your nights, eh?"

McVey said mildly, "Where's the old one?"

She jerked her head at a closed door to her back, not taking her dark eyes from him. He started to move past her, but she struck angrily at his shoulder. "Regard me, Carlos. I have no need to be spare-time woman. There are plenty of men including *Americanos* who—"

"Shut up," he said gently, watching her.

Her hard, flippant expression softened; she whispered his name. He smiled and took her into his arms. His lips brushed her shut eyes, a cheek and ear, and the smooth joining of neck and shoulder. She threw back her head, lips parted. His mouth found hers, roughly, as he put the residue of his thwarted anger at Virginia Gilchrist into the kiss. Abrana drew back in his arms, her eyes smoky with pride and passion and her own anger.

"Don' toy with me, Carlos." She glanced at the side door to her parents' room, and lowered her voice. "If you don' want a greaser girl even spare time . . ."

"Did I say so? But I've business on my mind, *querida mía.*" He thought detachedly that she set a man's blood afire as a pleasant diversion, but he had drawn an iron line short of the mounting jealousy of Mextown's young males, angry at a gringo's success with their fairest. He'd had to confine his visits to the dark, when a sudden anonymous knife-thrust would be too easy . . . and a poor and ignorant Mexican wench had no place in his plans.

Yet her loveliness was undeniably fine-bred and delicate; old Ysidro Ortega boasted of pure Castilian descent, and his granddaughter, with her blue-black hair and ivory skin, seemed to bear it out. Above the low round neckline of her blouse, fitful lamplight turned the skin to tawny satin and laid soft shadow in the beginning hollow between the small, pointed breasts. But his face tightened at the sight of the small crucifix gleaming coldly against the warm flesh. In sudden rage he wanted to tear it from her neck.

It framed a cold, hard remembrance of his mother. After his father's death she'd enforced a religious regimen of morning prayers, evening prayers, graces before and after every meal, till the numb ache of his knees filled every interval. The tedious Sunday sermons were nothing by comparison, but the gaunt sobersides of a preacher came regularly for free suppers, afterward discussing for hours hellfire and last things till you wanted to retch. Some ingrained habit of duty had held him, but the war had come as a welcome relief, sending him off with a passing guerrilla band at seventeen and with his mother's blessing; he was leaving her to kill Yankees, devil's spawn.

"Carlos?" Abrana's soft wonderment straightened his bitterly twisted grin into a charming smile. He moved her gently aside. "Later."

McVey opened the door to old Ysidro Ortega's long, narrow alcove of a room, closed it behind him. A wall-bracketed candle thick as a man's wrist flickered long weird shadows against the rough clay walls. The only furniture was a half-log table with a single bench, and a low wooden bedframe criss crossed with a network of rawhide thongs for a mattress. Reclining on this was Ysidro Ortega, eyes closed, frail chest barely astir with his breathing. On the foot of the bed perched a large, beady-eyed raven. It ruffled its inky plumage as old Ysidro opened one eye, glanced at McVey.

"I want you to look at something, *viejo*." McVey drew the document from his pocket, unwrapped it, and laid it on the table. Old Ysidro swung very slowly to his feet, yawned prodigiously, scratched his wispy gray ruff of hair, and made an odd little "Ch, ch," in his throat. The raven flapped up to his shoulder as Ysidro came to the table, seated himself. "It is late to be rousing an old man's bones, Eugenio," he told the raven. His voice was the rustle of dry corn shucks.

McVey leaned his fists on the table. "That's supposed to be the original king's charter for the Rivera grant. Look it over."

"Yes, very late, Eugenio," the old man crooned. McVey bridled with impatience. Ysidro yawned again and reached under his dirty cotton shirt to scratch his ribs. He was diminutive and shrunken, with a wrinkled, wizened monkey's face, and he must be incredibly old, McVey thought. . . . It was said he'd been past sixty when he sired Abrana's father. Like other strange tales revolving around this ancient man, it must be true. It was certainly true that he had a wide and enormous range of experience backed by an infallible memory, and McVey badly wanted his judgement on this document.

Ysidro finally dropped his bright black eyes to the charter, scanned it carelessly, and smiled. His yellow teeth were all intact and sound. "Have I not told you, Eugenio, that my ancestors were *conquistadores,* not blood of *los Indios?* Have I not told you—"

"Will you quit talking to that damned crow!" McVey grated. "All I want to know is whether that's the Rivera charter."

"Have I not told you, Eugenio," the old man went imperturbably, "that this McVey is a rooster without spurs? His soft crowing turns young girls' soft heads. McVey is getting mad, *amigo mío.* But he is not such a bird as your noble cousin, the fighting cock, he has no spurs, and the head of *el viejo* is old and hard."

Ysidro rose and went back to his bed. The raven dropped onto the bedpost, Ysidro stretched comfortably out. He crossed his hands on his chest and closed his eyes. He looked like a mummified saint's corpse till one sly sparkling eye cocked open in his shriveled parchment face.

"By the way, Eugenio, have I told you that I was a retainer on the estate of Jaime Sanchez y Nahuatl y Bandara y Rivera in my youth, and that because of my Castilian blood I became his personal valet?" His eye slid drowsily shut. "Yes, yes," he murmured, "I saw many times the charter given by the Spanish monarch to his family . . . and do you know, Eugenio, that *pergamino* on the table is the very same one?"

"*Gracias,* Eugenio," said McVey dryly, hiding his welling exultance. He returned the charter to its wrappings and his pocket, and left the room.

Abrana was standing by the outer door as he started for it, and she stepped quickly across his path, smiling up with childlike expectancy. He said mock-wearily, "All right, all right," and held out his arms. She nestled against him with a little giggling sigh. After a minute he let her go and started to open the door.

"*Vaya con Dios,* Carlos," she whispered. "I will pray for you to Our Lady. . . ."

"Save your Hail Mary's for grandpa, *querida* . . . needs 'em worse."

"*Abuelito* believes in nothing, but I do pray for him, I pray for everyone; it makes a good feeling in me. I wish you would pray sometimes, Carlos. I think the good God may hear it a Protestant man's way, though it is wrong."

"Damn it," he said viciously, "I've told you I got a crawful of that stuff from my old lady, get off it, will you!"

Her eyes blurred and her chin sank with a little sob. Why are you cruel to me? I have killed my pride, lost the respect of my family and friends. I have given up everything. For you. . . ."

He felt a twinge of guilt which died as quickly as it came. He stroked her head and whispered a little and left her smiling through her tears. He mounted and jogged back toward Blanco, his head full of excited speculations. Through it burned a savage and bitter satisfaction. His old lady, always talking about storing up treasures for the kingdom of heaven . . . he would show her and all of them, Virginia, Abrana, *women,* what a man could do on this earth without any damned women, reforming or cold or cloying, around him.

As he neared the fork where the river route joined the town road, the sound of two horses approaching from the other fork made him draw cautiously off behind a thicket. No telling who might be riding this lonely road at such an hour. He strained his eyes to pick out the riders in the moonlight—a big, broad pair riding abreast. He couldn't distinguish their features, but he thought that the larger man was Owen Rutledge—no mistaking that height and shoulder-breadth.

McVey waited several minutes after they'd ridden on, then put his horse into motion. What had brought Rutledge back to town, and at this time of night? A cold finger of fear touched his spine. Could Rutledge have found out something from Colonel M'Kandless that would enable him to learn the identity of the real charter thief? *Hell, you're spooking yourself, what could he know?* Yet McVey waited a full five minutes till they had ridden on, before putting his billy horse into motion.

As he rode down the silent main street, McVey saw Rutledge again, alone now, walking upstreet from the livery barn . . . passing up the hotel. *He'll be going to see Virginia then,* McVey thought, knowing real panic now. This late visit must mean that Rutledge had learned something. Passing the man, he swerved deep into the shadows at the opposite side of the street. Breathing easier, he rode on to the livery.

He turned in at the arched entrance, rode down the runway, stepped down from his saddle. He glanced about to see the squat man who'd ridden in with Rutledge, his back to McVey as he hoisted a pair of hulls onto the saddle pole. The lawyer gave him a fleeting wary and curious glance, then looked for the night hostler who was not in sight. A lamp burned in the window of the little walled-in office at the back of the barn.

"Oh, Bill!" he called. "Come out and take my horse."

The squat man turned casually and then stiffened, and the light from the bull's-eye lantern hanging on a stall post caught full on his shining black face. He simply stared at McVey and did not move.

"What's the matter with you, fellow?" McVey said irritably.

"I knows you," the Negro said simply, "Mistuh Sykes."

Terror rose and clawed up McVey's throat as a thick gasp. No . . . not after all these years. It could not be happening.

The Negro advanced with his great bulk rolling, his

long arms spread a little. McVey had more courage than most men, but in this moment he backed away till a stall partition caught him in the back. His voice was a thin squeak: "I don't know you. . . ."

"Why, you wouldn', Mistuh Sykes," the Negro said with a slight, almost dreamy, smile playing on his wide lips. "Been a good long time since I jumped on you after you killed my woman Saph . . . an' your boys put all that lead into me." His big hands lifted and caught McVey by the lapels. McVey shrank against the boards, thinking that there was something terrifyingly familiar in the Negro's words, and then the Negro said gently and gravely: "Not yet, Mistuh Sykes. First Mars' Owen will want—"

Owen, Rutledge—Rutledge! The name burst across McVey's memory. A few days after the war . . . a big farm with a family named Rutledge . . . this big black man . . . it all came frighteningly clear.

In wild panic he struggled, kicked and clawed at this captor. The Negro held him as if he were a child, forcing him into the runway. Another, more immediate memory coldly touched McVey's brain . . . he quit struggling, slipped his hand into his right coat pocket till it closed over the little pocket pistol. The Negro swung him face to face. "That's wise, white trash. You come 'long quiet, now—"

McVey tilted the pistol inside his pocket till it angled up at the broad chest a foot away. The Negro's gaze moved quickly to the bulging cloth, and then the gun made its spiteful bark, point-blank.

The Negro shuddered, his fists wrenched convulsively at McVey's lapels. He went down, hauling the lawyer with him. McVey got his knees under him and shot again, carefully, into the Negro's head.

"Sweet bleedin' Christ. . . ."

It was the hostler, standing in the entrance of his office, frozen by what he saw. McVey scrambled to his feet and lunged stumbling toward his horse. He got a toe in the stirrup and kicked the animal into a run before he was firmly in the saddle.

SEVEN

Leaving Abner to see to the horses, Owen headed for Virginia Gilchrist's little house. He saw lamplight in the front window, hesitated, unwilling at this late hour to interrupt her preparations for bed. *Get it over with,* he thought resignedly; *she won't like this any more than you do.* He went up the path and rapped solidly, twice, at the door. Virginia answered at once, framed in the open doorway—a slim and petite figure in an oft-washed skyblue dress which, he noticed, matched her vivid eyes.

"Why, Mr. Rutledge." She stepped aside and he entered, stiffly removing his hat. "Please have a chair. There's coffee—"

"No, ma'am," he said coolly, and added, "Thank you." He scowled down at his hat, looked up into her still, expectant face. "Miss Gilchrist, I've been to Lionclaw, and you can keep your fifty dollars."

She caught her lower lip in her teeth, her bewildered chagrin plain. "You've . . . changed your mind?"

"Yes'm. Colonel M'Kandless is no thief. You wouldn't understand, but—"

"No," she cut in coldly, "I don't understand. But your tone indicates plainly that your mind is made up. Very well." She stepped to the door and opened it, proudly waiting for him to leave.

He felt an abrupt respect for this girl's lonely, rock-ribbed poise. "Look—" He did not know what to say. Then words came with unintentional roughness. "Ma'am, how well do you know this McVey—the lawyer fellow?"

"That is quite clearly none of your business."

"No'm." He set his hat on and went out the door, turning on the threshold. "It's yours, though. And I advise you to think about that." He hesitated. "If you'll want to see me again, I'm taking a room at the hotel."

"And your friend? Abner? Is he sleeping at the hotel, too?"

The mocking scorn was in her words, not in their quiet tonelessness. He felt the blood crawl into his face. She was hurt, and she wanted to hurt back. He said matter-of-factly: "Abner will sleep in the stable. As he always does." Before she could counter, he said, "Good night," and headed swiftly down the path.

He heard the door close firmly on her parting mockery: "Good night, Mars' Rutledge."

His anger cooled to a rueful smile before he had reached the gate. She had an unexpected spirit behind that tart, prim front, he realized with a small, odd pleasure.

As he turned down the street, a gunshot brought Owen to a halt. A second shot cracked on its heel. A small caliber gun . . . and he placed its sharp reports near the livery barn. As he started into a long loping run, he saw a rider swerve out of the livery archway two blocks down. Low-bent in the saddle, lashing his horse north from town at an all-out run.

An unbidden fear took sharp hold on Owen. The breath tore in his chest as he lengthened stride. He ran breathlessly into the runway and there drew to a dead halt.

The lank hostler was bending over a sprawled form, and Owen ran to it, shoving the man aside. "Ab— *Abner*."

"Big man, this *negra's* dead," the hostler whispered in a low, awed way. ". . . Was back in the office. Heard the shot. Came out just as he pumped the second into his—"

Owen grabbed the man by the collar, twisted it savagely. "Who was it?"

"God's sake—man—chokin' me—" Owen released him, and the hostler rubbed his windpipe, eying him fearfully. "It was that shyster . . . McVey. Charlie McVey."

Owen dropped on his knees beside Abner, gently turning his head. His hand came away slippery . . . there was little blood. Numbly he opened the Negro's shirt. The first bullet had entered his chest squarely. It had, Owen noticed obscurely, cut clean through the rabbit's foot talisman, almost halving it. *It had to be broken that way, didn't it?*

A scrape of bootsteps brought his glance slowly around to the approaching gaunt and towering form of Matthew Claiborne. Others crowding behind him. Claiborne frowned and took a twisted cheroot from his bearded lips. "Your man Friday, eh? Well, I warned you not to stay around the basin."

Owen came to his feet, weight set on his toes. Bloody Matt, abruptly seeing a very real danger here, backed off a step. "You wouldn't," Owen said, almost whispering it, "have put McVey up to this, would you?"

Claiborne drew quickly on his cigar, watching Owen warily. "McVey the lawyer? . . . I've never met the fellow. Use your head, Rutledge. Would I set up a clumsy, needless killing like this?"

Owen shook his head gently. "Not your way. Unless you have some end I don't rightly see . . . yet."

"See here," Claiborne said uneasily. "I understand your feelings, but you can't bull about wildly accusing—"

Owen's violent swing-around broke him off. Owen bent and carefully gathered Abner into his arms. He started toward the archway, and Claiborne, with a soft oath, barely stepped from his path in time. Owen did not look at him or the others as they cleared his way. He turned down the boardwalk and halted after a few steps. *What now?* he thought emptily. *What next?*

There was a soft tap-tap of brisk steps coming . . . halting before him. He dragged his stare up to Virginia Gilchrist's face, white and wide-eyed in the feeble moonlight. "Oh, Owen . . . Owen. I'm sorry. He is—" She said then very softly, "He will spend this night under my roof. Come along."

She walked off a few paces, turned when he remained unmoving. "Please," she said gently.

He followed her in silence, his eyes fixed on her small, shawl-wrapped shoulders. Inside her parlor he laid Abner on the divan. He stood there a long time till his mind began to numbly function, feeling this last link with his past broken.

He realized that she was speaking, hesitantly. "I—didn't know him, of course, but I think—he must have been a kind of symbol—of dignity—of not only his own race, but of men everywhere who face out their condition no matter how all odds are against them. He—he looked like that kind."

Her words seemed to trigger loose the blind wrathful grief in him. *These damned cold-fish idealists. They think a man's feelings are something to be tacked on display for philosophical analysis. Christ!* He stared at her bitterly. "Abner was my friend." The words came strangely to his lips, before he was aware of what he'd said.

"Why," Virginia said softly, "that is all there is to say."

His anger slowly ebbed; he hadn't meant to use her as its target. He realized she had spoken unwillingly, for the comfort her words might give. "I . . ." He stopped, tiredly reflecting a moment. "I will appreciate your making the proper arrangements for a burial. I will be gone a while." He rubbed his eyes and re-fixed his attention. "Were you coming after me . . . back there?"

She nodded somberly. "I wanted to tell you I was sorry for how I reacted. . . . I know you meant well . . . but you were wrong, too—I mean about Charlie—" She broke off at what she saw in his face, then whispered, "What is it?"

"McVey," he pronounced distantly, tonelessly. "Your very good friend McVey. The hostler saw him put a second bullet into Abner's head. I do not think that was an accident, do you, Miss Gilchrist?"

As she stood in shocked silence he tramped past her to the door and went out, not closing it. He heard her wild cry behind him. "But why? *Owen, why?*"

He had claimed his bay at the livery and was jogging

along the north road before his chaotic thoughts caught up with Virginia's last words. Why? Why should a young lawyer struggling to build a respectable practice destroy his future with a cold-blooded murder? Certainly he hadn't provoked the shooting, and Abner would have provoked it for one reason only.

Abner had recognized Tierney or Sykes.

Mechanically Owen superimposed the description of John Sykes on the smiling cherub's face of Charles McVey. Remove the bristling yellow beard sported by Tierney's lieutenant . . . add seven years of age and a cultivated elegance and diction, and you had Red John Sykes: guerrilla, thief, and murderer.

McVey reached Lionclaw headquarters by midnight, and pulled off the ranch road well short of the Mexican shanties on the west end of the layout, for fear of being picked up by their dogs. He swung wide on the moonlit grass flats to come in on the headquarters from the north side. He put the billy horse into a dense cotton-wood grove back of the hayshed and here dismounted, tethering the animal.

He ran his hand over its wet, trembling flank. The horse was shuddering and breathing brokenly; he'd almost killed it in his haste to get here. After McVey's first ungoverned terror and the crushing realization that the game was up here, he was reasoning coolly. The basin people probably would not hunt him, even have a dodger put out, for his killing a Negro . . . but the Negro was Rutledge's man, and Rutledge would follow him to hell and back. In this cold and utter certainty, he needed help, and now. He had only the thin clothes on his back, an empty gun, no food, and a horse that could take him no further.

He left the grove and widely skirted the corrals and outsheds, taking in the bunkhouse and main house. All windows were dark, except for a solitary light burning in a first floor window of the big house. *That's Reed's room,* he thought exultantly, and breathed easier as he crossed the lawn at a fast trot.

He sidled cautiously to the lighted window. Reed M'Kandless sat in an overstuffed chair pulled close to a roaring fireplace. He wore a quilted dressing gown and his iron-rimmed glasses. He was reading.

McVey tapped on a pane. Reed turned in his chair, frowning as he removed his glasses. Then he came to the window, his eyes widening in recognition of McVey; his lips formed an angry question. McVey curtly signaled him to open the window. Reed wrestled up the sash, and McVey snapped, "Out of the way, I'm coming in," as he slung a leg over the sill. He stepped inside, closed the window, glanced narrowly around the big room, at the oaken commode and four-poster bed.

"Got it soft, haven't you, Cush?"

"Damn you, don't ever call me that!" Reed hissed. He dragged in a deep breath and said more steadily, "I told you never to come see me here. It better be important."

"To me, it is. To you too. Better listen."

Reed paced slowly back to his chair and laid his book down, then went to lean an arm on the fireplace mantel as he listened with a deepening frown. When McVey had finished, Reed thoughtfully took out a silk handkerchief, blew on his glasses, and squinted at the lenses as he polished them. He said without looking at McVey, "That's hardly news. Rutledge's family and mine lived far apart in Kentucky. The colonel did serve with Rutledge's father in the Kentucky legislature; that is our only connection—fortunately. He didn't know me from Adam."

"But I just killed his nigger," McVey said impatiently.

"So you said," Reed observed coldly. "Why tell me, though?"

"I need some things—food, a gun, some heavy clothes, a fresh horse. And money."

"So," Reed said with a half-smile. "So far my neck's safe, Charlie; why should I risk it by helping you?"

McVey moved to the vacated armchair and sank back into it with a sigh. He leaned his elbows on his stomach and steepled his fingers, regarding Reed with arrogant confidence. "Here's the thing, Reed. Any number of men could answer to our basic descriptions . . . and we've both changed in seven years. But you've guessed by now that Rutledge might not have come to this basin by chance. He might have got a clue—might have caught up with Garvey."

"How could Garvey tell him where to find us?" Reed demanded waspishly.

"Garvey came to Blanco Basin a year ago—evidently, like me, in hopes of getting money from your—from Mrs. M'Kandless. He happened to spot me in town, and I had to satisfy his curiosity. Then I gave him a little money, told him to ride on, forget what he'd seen and heard. Garvey was straight in his way, wouldn't have talked unless Rutledge cornered him. However that may be, only the Negro could positively identify us. The hostler saw me shoot him, so Rutledge'll be breathing down my neck shortly. With the Negro dead, your hide will be safe . . . unless Rutledge should catch up with me. Then I'll have him breathing down your neck. Simple?"

Reed swung from the fireplace, his face twitching. "You baby-faced bastard," he whispered. "For two years I've regretted the day I stopped at your mother's farmhouse . . . and invited a snot-nosed kid to come off to the war with me. I should have shot you when you found me here —forced me to set you up for a law practice—"

"But you first met the snot-nosed kid eleven years ago," McVey observed, "and filled his empty head with the glories of the great cause. We both got cynical fast after that. You taught me a lot, Reed . . . I'm going to repay the favor by clearing out of your life for good. With enough gold to throw Rutledge off my trail and get me to Canada. . . ." He shrugged. "It's to your interest to see I escape. Or the two of us can wait here for Rutledge, as you like—"

Reed cursed him once, softly and viciously, then strode to the commode and jerked open a drawer. He drew out a small canvas bag, threw it on the floor with a musical jangle. "There's forty double-eagles in there. Here," he savagely yanked out a holstered revolver wrapped in its cartridge belt, "is your gun. I can't get grub; the cook has his cot in the pantry. But there's a place in the mountains about twenty miles east of here. . . ."

"Sunfire?" McVey asked, and when Reed nodded, he added flatly, "I've heard of it. A dead mining camp, with a store and bar kept in business by the long riders—rustlers, killers, what-not—drifting through."

"Why, those are our people," Reed observed dryly. "What better can you ask? You ought to make it in a day . . . a place to sleep, a hot meal, and every man in the place ready to lie about you to Rutledge, throw him off your trail."

McVey smiled thinly as he strapped on the gunbelt. "I need a heavy coat. It's cold in the high country."

"Just a minute." M'Kandless went to the door, opened it, looked warily up and down the corridor, then stepped out. In two minutes he returned with a frayed mackinaw over his arm. He chucked it at McVey.

"Thank you, Reed." The lawyer started to pull on the thick coat, but it bound around his shoulders. With a curse he shed it, shrugged out of his suitcoat, and afterward strained into the mackinaw.

"It's an old one of Cissie's," Reed M'Kandless said with an amused malice, "but you're not much bigger'n her."

Reed did not answer, buttoning the mackinaw to his neck. He picked up his suitcoat and transferred his pocket pistol to the mackinaw. He glanced quickly at Reed and hesitated before he drew the cloth-wrapped Rivera charter from the coat and hurriedly thrust it into his trousers pocket.

"What's that?"

McVey met the sly interest in Reed's tone with a sharp, "Nothing," between his teeth.

"You act damn chinchy about 'nothing'."

McVey hesitated again, thought with a smile, *why not?* "This is the Rivera charter. I borrowed it from Miss Virginia Gilchrist . . . for reasons which aren't important now. It just struck me that a man of your abilities might find a way to use it. How much would it be worth to you, Reed?"

"Not a damned thing, friend," Reed said with a laugh.

"The Gilchrist woman tried to take the trusting old colonel in with that thing . . . even he wasn't simple enough to fall for such an obvious fake."

"Fake?" McVey asked softly. "Have you heard of Ysidro Ortega?"

Reed frowned. "Who hasn't? Old fellow over in Mextown, old as Methuselah and nearly as wise. He's a local legend."

"I saw him tonight before the trouble. Ysidro spent years under this roof when it belonged to the Riveras . . . and he says that's the original king's charter."

"I see." Reed stroked his spade beard. "And you were going to use it to shake down the colonel—or another interested party?" McVey did not answer, watching Reed's face as he paced a slow circle, seeing it shade from thoughtfulness to calculation, and McVey thought: *He's still Cushing Tierney at heart.*

Reed abruptly turned to face him. "You have all my ready cash in those double eagles. But listen—"

"No notes, no promises," McVey said flatly. "I've got to clear out now, and I won't be back. . . . In that case, I'll hang on to the document—and take the chance that I may be able to use it someday. Now I want a horse."

Impatience was beginning to ride him as M'Kandless studied him for a cold, silent moment, and he derived only thin amusement from the leashed hatred in Reed's eyes. "All right," Reed said then. "You came here on one, I suppose?"

"Left him in the grove back of the hayshed, near windbroken."

Reed nodded curtly. "Get back there and wait. I'll try to get you a fresh one from the corrals without rousing anybody—"

"If you rouse anybody," McVey cut him off softly, "I'll have to break on a winded horse, in which case the federals learn where you are. You get that horse, and get him quiet—Cushing."

EIGHT

Owen came stiffly up off his haunches, shifting his shoulders against the sweaty cling of his calico shirt. The sun had broiled up over the east peaks an hour past, and his legs ached from many such stops to examine signs in the road still mud-roiled from the heavy rain two nights ago.

He wiped his sleeve across his face, let his arm drop, a tired gesture. Last night he had not gone far from Blanco town before coming to the first fork-off. He was no tracker; in vague moonlight it had been difficult picking out McVey's fresh trail at the proper turn. Lionclaw had its own maze of ancient range roads, with a number of turn-offs to the small ranches strung along the south basin. Thus he'd made slow headway till false dawn.

He had noted earlier that McVey's track seemed to make for Lionclaw along the straight-ruled route he and Abner had traveled, on directions from the livery hostler. But Lionclaw was surely not McVey's goal and he could have turned off anywhere. Daylight had found Owen deep in Lionclaw range, less than two miles from its headquarters, and still he moved at an inchmeal pace rather than risk losing McVey.

Now he mounted his bay after the last ground-check and went slowly on, leaning from his saddle to scan the road beneath. Strained eyes and muscles, lack of sleep, were taking their iron toll; with these, a weighted despair. It was evident that McVey had pushed his animal hard, and all the while and still, he was widening many hours' lead. *This is no good, should have asked for a posse of men who know the country. And where,* he thought sinkingly, *will you find a posse to run down a black* 'man's killer? Besides—pride, rage, grief, call-it-what-you-might—goaded him to run down Abner's murderer alone. And he had time now, plenty of time; he had that much.

A brisk-pacing horse coming up from the long flats ahead caused him to slow and loosen the Navy Colt in its holster. Within five minutes Cissie M'Kandless reined in her sorrel by him stirrup to stirrup.

He touched his hat, saying distantly, "An early jaunt, Miss Cissie?"

The girl's face was deeply flushed; she wore the same gray riding habit she had yesterday, and the wind toiled with and loosened wisps of hair from beneath her narrow-brimmed hat. She removed the hat and dangled it from her hand by the chin-strap, avoiding his eyes in deep confusion. "I like to ride early in the morning. I usually do. That is—"

"Know McVey, the lawyer?"

Her head tipped up at his point-blank question. "Why, certainly . . . by sight."

"Seen him?"

"This morning, you mean? No-o . . . should I have?" Her direct gaze was puzzled.

Owen let out a heavy breath. "McVey killed Abner. Last night. I'm trying to find him."

"Killed—Abner? The Negro?" she asked disbelievingly, and when he nodded: "I—I'm sorry. But I don't understand. . . ."

"And no time to explain. Will you trust me?"

"I think," she said softly, "I would trust you for anything."

"McVey's tracks lead to your ranch. That makes no sense to me."

She shook her head with an emphatic, "He didn't come by our place, Mr. Rutledge."

"Then where would a man go, knowing he'd be followed?" His voice was edged with impatience.

She thought only a moment. "Sunfire. That's an old mining town back in the mountains, well past Lionclaw's boundaries. A flash-in-the-pan gold camp in the big rush of '68. I've heard the men say it's a hangout for all sorts of drifting riffraff. A man named Bayliss runs a saloon and store there—the only stopover for men going over that arm of the mountains. Then, the only good trail through goes past Sunfire. A man would almost certainly stop . . ."

"And how would he get there?" Head bent, he listened to her directions, said gravely, "Thank you, Miss Cissie." He started to rein past her, and she reached and caught his rein in a strong, slim hand; he saw her face pale beneath its tan.

"I'll talk to Pa—get some men to help. You can't go there alone."

"That's how I've got to go."

She shook her head bitterly, straightened in the saddle. "I'll never understand men. Well, then—"

His face relaxed with the faintest smile. "At least be careful?"

"Yes," she said, and did not smile. "I think that—I wish—" She bit her lip, watching him a still moment, her eyes tender and worried. "Goodbye, Mr. Rutledge."

He rode on, the brief gentleness she'd touched in him hardening again. What had she almost said? Perhaps that she had fallen in love with him, he thought with a quiet pity now. No doubt she thought so—with a stranger who had saved her father's life and shown a gentle, brief understanding of her confused youth. Maybe being lonely and young and too-sheltered was worse in its way than the bruising, bitter clashes with life which had drained away his green years.

Toward sunset Owen rode over a hump of the rocky pass he had followed from the low plains, and a bare mile ahead saw a slapdash clutter of shacks that was Sunfire. The town had been hastily thrown up, unpainted, neglected, soon abandoned to the raw mountain elements. The road crawled like a torpid snake down between the buildings and onward.

On one side rose a mountain flank scarred with old gold diggings that showed how quickly the camp had birthed and died; opposite, a castellated bulge of lava lifted majestically above the tawdry buildings, and Owen saw how Sunfire had taken its name. Some hardrock miner with a touch of poetry in his soul had come over this pass at sunset, just as the dying light crowned the lava bulge with orange fire and bled streamers of molten gold down its ribbed corrugations.

In fifteen minutes he dismounted in front of a clap-boarded building in sad disrepair, its weathered shakes flapping loosely in a hard wind that lashed eddies of dust up the deserted street. It was by far the most imposing structure still standing, wide and two-storied, with a crudely lettered sign—

GRUB LIKUR SUPLYS SLEEP—DOLER NITE

—above its sagging porch. Two horses, leaning hipshot to windward, were tied at the rail. Owen regarded them narrowly as he tied the bay . . . neither was the short-coupled horse the Blanco hostler, whom he'd questioned, had told him was McVey's.

He tramped up on the porch, skirted a gaping hole in the rotten planks, and pushed through the batwing doors. The bar was a pair of unplaned two-by-sixes nailed across a couple of beer barrels. Two ragged men turned from it and gave him their dirty, shifty stares as he came up beside them. He ignored them, looking across at the bartender. He was a tremendously fat old man wearing greasy leather pants supported by red galluses over his dirty cotton underwear. His frosty eyes glinted without expression above a tangled gray ambush of whiskers.

"You Bayliss?"

The cold eyes shifted sparely. "I'm Sam Bayliss." His voice grated like a rusty bucksaw. "Yours?"

"Feed, a stall for my horse. A meal. A bed."

"All right. Whiskey?"

Owen nodded. Bayliss set out a use-yellowed glass and took a labelless bottle from the two-by-six backbar. He poised it above the glass but didn't pour, his hard glance questioning. Owen sighed and laid a coin on the bar. The drink drained the bottle. Bayliss gave its bot-

tom three hard raps against the wall. He turned to meet
Owen's narrow look with a toneless, "Tellin' my old
woman to set another plate." He skirted the bar and went
out the batwings. Owen heard him lead the bay up a side
alley, evidently to a stable in the rear.

He took his drink, hearing stealthy feet mounting stairs
above his head. Aware of the drifter pair's suspicious
glances, Owen walked around the bar and went announced through the back door, halting on its threshold. A slatternly, tired-looking woman was turning sizzling steaks in a skillet; she said without looking up, "Want
sump'n?"

Owen looked bleakly at the oilcloth-covered table, seeing the tin plate with a half-eaten steak and the half-empty
coffee cup. He looked at the woman, watching him now
with a faint uneasiness.

"Supper," he said.

Her thin reddened hand touched the bosom of her
soiled dress and pushed back a straggle of lank hair from
her face. "Sit yourself. Ready in a minute." She picked
up the dirty dishes and clattered them into a wreckpan.

Bayliss came in, then the drifters, and the four of them
hunched in rickety chairs around the small table, wolfing
down beefsteak, fried potatoes, and scalding black coffee. The wordless silence was somehow deadly. Behind his
famished concentration on the food, Owen felt the di-
rected hostility of them all, and since his own rough appearance should have passed him without suspicion, he
knew that word had come ahead . . . there was Bayliss's
overt signal, that half-eaten meal, the quick footsteps
ascending the staircase which he now saw through a doorway to his right. He sized the situation, and did not like it,
and thought: *The drifters won't buy in. But Bayliss'll
back McVey; wait a while . . . watch him.*

Afterward he went back to the barroom and poured
another drink while the drifters started a stud game,
squatting over a barrelhead in the corner. Beyond the
fly-blown windows night had salved over the sun-
blistered buildings. Bayliss entered from the kitchen, his
frayed carpet slippers slap-slapping, bearing an armload

of cedar stove lengths which he dumped by the blackened fieldstone fireplace. He stoked up a fire, then came to stand behind the bar, not looking at Owen.

The spreading tawny glow beat back the high-country night chill, pleasantly thawed Owen's numbing body, and his thoughts drifted; he caught himself nodding, uneasily aware of a creeping drowsiness reminding him that he'd gone more than thirty hours without sleep—and prospect of a sleepless night ahead. His hand rasped over his short beard, rubbed his eyes. Thirty-five hours . . . since he and Abner had broken camp with North and Missou Holbrook two days ago. All that had happened since seemed unreal, a confused drift of nightmare scenes, and he knew this too was the dead weariness of mind and body.

He looked suddenly at Bayliss, seeing him watching with a crafty calculation, and he thought stolidly, *No, you beady-eyed bastard, I won't sleep, but you'll think otherwise, and that's fine*. He said aloud: "How about that bed?"

"Come along," Bayliss grated almost pleasantly. He lifted a lantern from a nail, lighted it, and led the way through the kitchen and up the narrow stairs. The lantern danced wavering shadows along the grimy walls and shafted through the murky corridor above. Owen glanced at the doors they passed, knowing McVey was behind one . . . listening . . . doubtless with a gun pointed at the door, ready to blast. *I'll wait, and he'll break,* Owen thought. *Sometime tonight he'll break.*

Bayliss halted by a door, saying, "No lock. Keep a shotgun by my bed. Sing out, anyone pesters you." Which was by way of an oblique warning, Owen knew. He waited till Bayliss turned away, then opened the door and went in, closing it.

He tossed his hat on the black shape of the narrow cot, cursed as he barked his shins getting around it to the window through which first moonlight thinly streamed. Holding his breath, he silently forced up the warped sash. He shivered at the inrush of icy air.

He pulled up a stool which, with the bed, constituted

the room's sole furniture. He huddled deeper into his sheepskin, leaned his crossed arms on the sill with the Navy Colt in his lap . . . settled in chilled alertness to wait.

NINE

Backing the town on either side rose the mountain-flank and the lava heights. Only a man afoot could tackle either. McVey would not leave afoot. That left the road, and from his window Owen had a clear view of its moon-paled ribbon. Time passed, and his rigid body relaxed to the hypnotic creaking of building timbers in a high wind, the ruffled slap of loose shakes on the roof. Twice he nodded, each time jerked erect, again settled back.

Think of something. He thought of Virginia Gilchrist, remembering her face, her movements and voice with a small, odd excitement that kept him awake a time. But his head bowed slowly against his arms; he dozed, his thread of awareness raveled out exhaustedly without quite letting go. . . .

He jerked upright, suddenly on his feet . . . listening. Above the thin moan of wind, he heard the creak of stairboards. *He's left his room, he's going down.* Owen's muscles jerked with the impulse to follow; he remembered Bayliss and the shotgun. *He's like to cut loose, first sight of you. Wait . . . cover the road.*

Owen sank on his haunches by the window. He heard the swing doors creak open beneath the porch—Bayliss' low voice. The hurried rasp of feet turning up the adjoining alley. Owen waited with an iron patience. Shortly he heard the rapid tattoo of hoofbeats alongside the building, and the wicked tension uncoiled in him. He cocked his revolver.

He leaned from the window as McVey swerved out of

the alley, bent low in his saddle, heels drumming the horse's flanks . . . a big, rangy buckskin, not the horse on which he'd left Blanco, Owen noted detachedly as he braced the Navy Colt across his forearm—fired.

The buckskin shuddered and broke stride. Owen shot again as it came abreast of his window.

Realizing that he had lost all control over the animal, McVey had freed his feet from the stirrups, plunging into the dust in a skidding sprawl. He crawled slowly to his hands and knees, doggedly shaking his head. His gun had fallen from its holster and he looked around for it and floundered over to it. Owen held his fire, thinking coldly, *He knows where Cushing Tierney is. First things first.*

He let out his breath in a shout: "Rutledge here, Sykes . . . throw the gun away!"

McVey pivoted on a hip with incredible swiftness, at the same time palming up his gun from the dust. He fired blindly at the window, then was on his feet racing for the alley. His slug hammered into the weathered clapboards. Owen tilted the Navy gun to bear on McVey's legs. He shot carefully, and missed, and then McVey vanished into the areaway.

With a savage curse Owen spun from the window, wrenched the door open. He pounded through the black corridor and down the stairwell. Veering hard at the midway landing where the stairs turned at a right angle, he ran full into the blaze of a lamp in Bayliss' right hand—shotgun in his left as he huffed up the stairs.

Owen lunged at him without breaking pace, lowering his shoulder to slam full into Bayliss' chest. The fat man arched over backward as though catapulted, somersaulting helplessly down the steep-pitched stairwell. The impact of his fall shook the building. The lamp arced up and down and broke, sending a streamer of oil-fed flame across the bottom landing and Bayliss' legs. Bayliss howled and rolled ponderously, beating wildly at his pants. Owen vaulted the blazing floor and ran across the kitchen and out the back door.

As he flung it open, went through, a purple-orange

tongue of flame licked from the darkness. Owen leaped sideways, out of the framing light. He fired at the gun-flash, heard the pound of retreating feet.

For a moment he crouched against the clapboards, hearing the harsh sweep of his own breathing, accustoming his eyes to the shadows that steeped the deep vale of back yard. He made out a low silhouette of the stables, its wide-thrown double doors from which the shot had come.

He left the wall, legs driving at the clay ground as he went across the compound. He came with an aching slam against the stable wall by the doorframe as from deep in the building, McVey shot again. Owen fired back and then dived inside in a low-running lunge. His head crashed against an unseen stall partition, and his foot slipped and he fell with a grunt on his belly. He lay for a dazed moment in the straw-dung-and-ammoniac reek of the damp dirt floor. Then twisted around to strain his eyes toward the stall cornerpost. He saw nothing but moonlight-jagged cracks in the warped wall-boards. A horse whickered and stamped in a stall farther down. There was an on-run of silence beneath the low wail of wind.

Owen pulled himself soundlessly to his hunkers, began shucking out the spent loads in his gun. He fumbled for fresh cartridges and thumbed them into the chambers—cocked the gun.

McVey fired at the sound. His bullet ripped through the stall boards, off-target by a good two feet. Owen crouched and listened. He heard faint noises at the stable rear, and he thrust his gun around the upright and fired. The noises continued—a steady up-moving grate of feet on wood that was baffling. Next a rustle of straw just beneath the roof; then, understanding: *He went up a ladder to the loft.* Straining his eyes, Owen distinguished the two-feet-square outline of the traphole against the lesser gloom of the ceiling. *He'll wait for a good shot—cut down from there.* Owen considered that momentarily. *He's used four loads. Give him his shot.*

Owen rose slowly, steadied himself with a hand on the

partition, stepped into the areaway faintly illumined from the open doors. He took a tentative step forward. At the faintest whisper of sound, he stepped sideways into shadow; McVey's gun bellowed. Owen waited for a half-crouched instant of silence. A reek of powderfumes drifted the air. He guessed that McVey did not know whether he'd made a hit.

"All right, Red John," he said softly. "You were enough of a horseman once to keep your hammer on a dead chamber. Come down or I come after you."

He knew a moment's shock as McVey's bitter curse mingled with the roar of McVey's gun. Unthinkingly he felt the wind of the slug as his own gun tilted to bear, bucked against his palm. McVey let out a choking, hard-hit grunt, his body rolled slackly across the trap-hole and, bent at the middle, fell through.

You shot too fast. Owen numbly sheathed his gun and groped forward till his foot touched McVey's body. He heard the low groan. He breathed almost a merciless prayer: *Stay alive, Red John. Just a while yet.*

He bent and gathered up the motionless form. It was spare and light and limp in his arms. He carried McVey outside and laid him in a patch of moonlight. He rolled McVey's head gently in one big palm. "You hear me, Sykes?"

McVey's head stirred; his eyes rolled open, glittered against the light. He coughed blood. His drained whisper was harsh: "Damn you . . . killed me, Rutledge. You've killed me."

"What I set out to do."

"I know . . . known it a long time. Knew it would catch up sometime. Funny how a man knows. Clean forgot though . . . had live shell . . . under pin." He coughed again, a retching and violent spasm. "You wanted me—alive—awhile?"

"Long enough to learn about Cushing Tierney. That long."

McVey managed a smile of wistful charm. "You big son of a bitch. Now you'll never know."

"Depends," Owen murmured, "on what you hate

more—me, or Tierney getting scot-free. There's still time."

"Why," Charlie McVey whispered smilingly, "That's so, and his name—his name is Reed M'Kandless now."

Owen shook his head soberly. "Won't work. You must have some grudge on him . . . telling me a man like Colonel M'Kandless would give a killer of women and children the protection of his name."

"He did!" It left McVey as a harsh cry. He choked again, sagged against Owen's arm; his breathing shallowed and seemed to thread away. For a moment Owen thought he was gone, then had to bend his head to catch McVey's broken whisper.

Cushing Tierney, he said, was Colonel M'Kandless' brother-in-law. The colonel's wife was still alive when Tierney had fled up from Texas, where Owen lost his trail years ago, evading the federal troops then swarming the country who'd have shot him on sight. In desperation he'd gone to his sister and begged her protection. Cushing had long been a prodigal problem of the highborn Tierneys, and inspired, as prodigals often did, perverse affection and protective loyalty in his clansmen.

Lila M'Kandless had heard stories of her brother's depredations and of course believed none of them. She had conceived the foolproof plan of passing Cushing off as her husband's brother. But even the colonel's almost reverent love for his wife, his inbred loyalty to his own class, his hatred of the Union, his ready admission as an old soldier that the bloody tales of war were largely wild exaggeration and propaganda, could not bring him to stomach this deception.

It was then that Tierney had desperately gambled all on one fact: that the colonel, like all the Southern aristocracy, placed the white females of their own families on a protective pedestal—a point of honor that took precedence over all else. He'd sought the colonel out privately and had threatened to inform the federals that his brother-in-law, the colonel, had already sheltered him for a month in return for the lion's share of the cash loot pillaged by Tierney's Raiders. As an outspoken enemy

of the Union, the very least the colonel might expect
from a federal judge was a lengthy prison sentence. To
leave his child and semi-invalid wife alone and helpless
was out of the question. His first alternative reaction
was to shoot Tierney on the spot—but the shock would
certainly kill his wife. Caught between a Scylla of deceit
and a Charybdis of dishonor, the colonel had chosen
deceit . . . had told his wife he'd agree.

As McVey talked, Owen's thoughts raced back over
the brief battle-glimpse he'd had of Tierney, the man's
description, and his leisurely view of Reed M'Kandless.
It could be . . . trim off the bushy burnsides of war-
time fashion, add a neatly clipped spade beard, pad
the tense-wiry body with the flesh and pallor of age and
soft living . . . and there emerged a sleek and slothful
stranger.

A short time following the wasting death of Mrs.
M'Kandless, from consumption, John Sykes, broke and
hungry after five years of riding a grubline following his
separation from Tierney in Texas, arrived in Blanco
Basin. Tierney had sometimes spoken of his sister, Mrs.
M'Kandless, and Sykes had come to Lionclaw in hopes
of wheedling money from her. Lila was in her grave by
then, but Sykes quickly recognized Reed M'Kandless as
the man at whose side he'd ridden through the war. A
single threat to anonymously notify the Territorial Marshal of Reed's identity had resulted in Reed's introducing
Sykes to Blanco Basin as an upstanding young lawyer
from his home town in Kentucky. A good suit and a
clean-shaven face, a quick and facile mind applied to
long study-hours over lawbooks, had filled out the new
guise of Charles McVey, attorney-at-law.

McVey's voice broke and sank and his eyes closed.
He whispered, "Get me a drink. Whiskey."

Owen swung his head toward the stealthy approach of
feet from behind. Bayliss halted flat-footed, a lantern
dangling from his hand. It glinted on his shotgun. Owen
said harshly, "It's done. Keep that Greener pointed
down."

Bayliss vaguely sleeved his slack mouth, uneasy stare

fixing the hard, battered face of the huge man crouching before him. "Sure. All right."

"Bring him a drink."

"Water?"

"No."

Bayliss nodded and shuffled away. Owen watched his back till the kitchen door closed behind him.

"Rutledge?" McVey's whisper was surprisingly strong, faintly mocking. "Glad we got your family," he husked. "Didn't kill your sisters right off, you know . . . Rutledge, you believe there's a Hell?"

There is no regret in him, Owen thought dismally, *even now.* "At times," he said aloud, yet softly, "I can hope so."

McVey's lips stirred in a soundless chuckle. "Ma . . . Ma, all that praying better do some good now . . . you old bat!" His body tensed, breath a dwindling rasp—he was motionless.

The wind rattled skeletons of dead brush against the stable wall. Owen shivered. He looked up as Bayliss, returning, extended the bottle. "Never mind," he said.

TEN

The five men left their horses a good two hundred yards from the Lionclaw outbuildings and went in on foot through the moonlight. At a word from Matthew Claiborne, his four companions halted in the deep shadow of the hay shed. Claiborne let out his breath and sleeved sweat from his face, though the windless night air bit strongly through his duck jacket. At midnight now, bunkhouse and main house lay in sleeping darkness.

Claiborne had already gone over the simple strategy several times; he repeated it now in a grating whisper,

looking hard at each man as though daring him to mis-
understand. "Danny, you and I handle the main house.
Other three take the bunkhouse. Blaize, light your lantern when you reach the bunkhouse, go in quickly, catch
them in its light, order them to lie still. You and Clay will
cover the crew while Lafferty collects their guns. Then
you report to me at the house. And Blaize—I want no
gunplay unless they start it; then, do not shoot to kill.
Understand me?"

Blaize inclined his head patiently. He was a tall, yellow-
haired Texan with cold, bleached eyes. The other three
drifters whom Claiborne had hired for this job were dregs
of the chuckline, caring for nothing but a fast, lazy, reckless dollar. Claiborne had approached them at random
among the saddle bums that drifted in and out of his
saloon. Yesterday he had selected Blaize more purpose-
fully from the same ilk. The Texan was as disreputable
and hardcase as any, but with a cool, efficient head, and
the others would take his orders. Claiborne needed one
man who would smoothly nullify the danger of Lionclaw's twenty-man crew while he himself directly
handled the M'Kandlesses. He wasn't concerned about the
shanty row of Mexican families not far distant; the Mexes
of Blanco Basin had never given more than nominal
loyalty to their American conquerors, caring little or
nothing in their *mañana* thoughts for the disputes of
the alien race they served.

They separated then, Blaize and his two men gliding
through the shadows toward the bunkhouse; Danny, squat
and barrel-built, huffed noisily behind the lofty form of
Claiborne, moving up the shallow, moon-bathed rise toward the big house. Claiborne had made only one visit
here, to show his old Armijo land grant to Colonel
M'Kandless, with the expected result of the colonel's or-
dering him off in rage. It had given Claiborne his chance
to size the layout of house and grounds.

Now as he and Danny skirted the house's west flank
to reach the kitchen door, he had only a bitter hope that
this would come off without a hitch. If Ivy North had suc-
ceeded in the one certain stroke that would have cut the

legs from under the opposition—killing Colonel M'Kand-less in a street duel—it would have been easy to deal with his daughter and brother by a few bold, brief threats—for Claiborne would stand no chance against the M'Kandless position if he matched his claim against their wealth in the courts. But the colonel's fragile body contained a steel will, and he wouldn't be caught twice by the same trick.

North would have had a sure thing if that damned Rutledge hadn't interfered, Claiborne thought bitterly . . . he shivered and cursed under his breath. If he weren't free of the puerile superstitious fancies of most men, he'd almost believe that Rutledge had the Indian sign on him. Three nights ago in the livery, when he'd let drop a casual taunt to Owen over the body of that *Negra,* he'd been for a moment a hair's breadth from death. Heaven help the man that Rutledge had marked for the Negro's killing. . . . But two days had passed; Rutledge hadn't re-turned, and Claiborne had breathed more easily. At this of all times, he wanted no outside interference from Rut-ledge or any other. Four days had passed since North's failure, time to lull the suspicions of Lionclaw people—and Claiborne was ready for the big step. Forcing the colonel off Lionclaw would lay the groundwork for crowding the old man to a compromise.

They had achieved the back door of the hacienda now, and Claiborne halted Danny with a word. He had brought two lanterns from town, given one to Blaize. He lighted the other, cupping his big bony hands to shield its glow. Holding it high, he silently lifted the doorlatch and stepped through. In the narrow pantry opening off the kitchen, the cook came instantly upright on his cot, blinking confusedly at the flare of light.

"Sit quiet, fella," Danny ordered in his deep, ugly voice, his gun leveled on the man. Bloody Matt did not wait for the cook's response; he moved on through the dining room, and from there into a wide corridor. The lantern flickered a murky glow which showed two closed doors on either wall. Bedrooms, one empty, three occupied . . . but which by whom? Claiborne halted for a nonplussed moment. The girl and Reed M'Kandless might offer token resistance . . . but it was the colonel who concerned him.

He stiffened, watching a pencil of light form beneath the near door on his right . . . then the stealthy creak of a floorboard. Someone had caught a sound—lighted a lamp and was coming to the door. Claiborne's heart pounded as he cocked his gun.

The door flung abruptly open. Colonel M'Kandless, his mane of hair rumpled over his thin, intent face, stood there in a dressing gown. He held a heavy pistol, swung it to bear as he saw Claiborne. There was no time for words. With a resigned sigh Claiborne fired.

The colonel's frail body spun against the doorjamb, his pistol and lamp clattering to the floor. The lamp landed upright without breaking, but its chimney cracked as the colonel's body sank down, pressing it against the jamb. Claiborne, watching him twitch a frail hand and become motionless, thought with weary dispassion that he'd just watched his thin hope for a smooth operation die stillborn.

The adjacent door was flung wide and Cissie M'Kandless came out, a wrapper thrown over her nightgown. She looked uncomprehendingly at Claiborne and then at her father, went down on her knees by him with a terrible cry. Reed M'Kandless stepped from his room opposite the colonel's, sleepily scratching his thinning tousled hair. He froze, hand in his hair, for the space of three seconds as he took it all in.

"You stand—" Claiborne began, when the girl came suddenly to her feet with a thin scream and flung herself at him. Claiborne took a backward step, backhanded her across the jaw with the hand that held his gun. She crumpled heavily at his feet without a sound. Claiborne lifted a sultry, wicked gaze to Reed M'Kandless. Reed slowly unfroze, one pudgy hand gently massaging the flannel nightshirt over his plump middle. "Oh no," he said stupidly.

"No," Claiborne said. "Unless you make one move." A muffled shot cracked out on the heel of his words.

From the bunkhouse, he thought, and cocked his head to listen. There was another shot. A long, waiting silence, before he relaxed.

"Now," he said conversationally, "are there keys to these bedrooms?"

Still rubbing his belly, open-mouthed and wide-eyed, Reed M'Kandless mechanically nodded. Then he said tonelessly, "A master key—in the colonel's desk."

"Get it."

Reed shuffled across the hallway, gave the colonel's body a quick shuddering glance as he went into the room and opened the single drawer of a small writing desk. Claiborne watched him from the doorway. "The key," Bloody Matt said gently, as Reed's hand dipped in the drawer. "Bring out just the key."

Reed shuddered again. He held up the key. Claiborne nodded. "Drag the body inside . . . take the girl back to her room. Lock both rooms."

"Then—?"

Claiborne smiled faintly. "Then we make medicine, you and I."

He saw the hall shadows change shape, quickly turned as Blaize came quietly into the hall beside him, lantern in hand. "How did it go?" Claiborne asked.

Blaize did not reply, his cold gaze warming wickedly as it touched the still form of the girl. "You hurt that woman?" he asked softly.

"She's not dead, I had to hit her," Claiborne said irritably, but he knew a brief cold wariness as the Texan's bleach eyes fixed him dispassionately. "Kill a man, take his ranch—but never lay a finger on a woman, eh, Blaize? You Texans—setting anything in calico on a pedestal—"

"You got objections, mister?" Blaize cut in softly. His gaze never left the girl as Reed awkwardly lifted her limp weight.

"Quit it," Claiborne said wearily. "I heard shots—"

"That segundo went after a gun. I powdered him off. Too bad, I made him to be a Texas man."

"Damn you. Is he dead?"

"Unh-unh. Side hit."

"The other shot?"

"Feisty little ranny name of Fitz. Jumped me. Lafferty winged him."

Claiborne slowly exhaled. Still, the colonel's death had fulfilled his pessimism. *That killing will make a very large stink,* he thought coldly. But he could not change what had happened, and it was too late to pull back.

"All right. Get back to the bunkhouse, take Danny and the cook with you. The four of you watch the crew."

Blaize hesitated. "You?"

"The girl will be locked in her room safely beyond my vile clutches," Claiborne answered dryly. "Don't worry . . . I'll conduct the rest of my business with her uncle."

Claiborne lighted a cheroot, took it from his lips and exhaled a fragrant streamer. He regarded Reed M'Kandless through the smoke a speculative moment, sailed the match into the woodbox, and said idly, "I meant to wound your brother. He died too easily."

They were sitting at a kitchen table now, facing each other across it with the slack poise of two wary tomcats, not yet tensed for battle. Claiborne had searched the house room by room for weapons, had found, besides the colonel's Colt, only a brace of antique dueling pistols above the parlor fireplace mantel. Satisfied that he could parley in safety, he'd ordered Reed into the kitchen.

He'd meant to frighten Reed M'Kandless into submissive agreement under his own terms, but already he was sensing that this stout, slack-bodied man's foppish appearance concealed a latent secretive shrewdness. Bloody Matt decided to walk soft at first and take the full measure of his man. He opened with a casual half-apology that yet held no jot of regret, because he knew Reed wouldn't be fooled.

Already Reed's first shocked paralysis had ebbed; his cool milky eyes made a wary sizing-up of Claiborne. He looked at the cocked revolver by Claiborne's elbow, and again, searchingly, at his enemy. "His doctor told the colonel his heart was going," he said mildly. "Any slight shock. . . ." He shrugged, and was silent.

Claiborne frowned. "You know what I want, M'Kandless. Lionclaw. I'm holding a sure hand—"

"That Armijo grant, yes," Reed interrupted, his tone faintly insolent. "But you set it up badly. I'm guessing that you hadn't counted on killing the colonel or Dirksen . . . just moving them and us all off Lionclaw to help cinch your position. . . . I'm guessing you're on a spot now, Claiborne, and singing soft."

"Not altogether, friend. One dead man—or twenty— tell no tales about another dead man."

"A bluff to back a losing hand," Reed jeered lightly. "Your only chance to get Lionclaw by legal murder was to have the colonel braced by that gunnie in town . . . that failed. Now you've started open murder, you have two choices: commit more murders that can't be concealed long, else make some sort of deal with me. Now —what's your offer?"

"Why, your life, damn you—what else?"

Reed gently shook his head, smiling. "Not enough. You thought to scare me—you're smart enough to see by now that it won't work."

Claiborne slacked back in his chair, studying the man. He said calmly: "All right. What's *your* offer?"

Reed said immediately, "I cover up the colonel's death. He had a heart attack before you came. Died of natural causes. That's the story that'll go out. No inquest, no legal stink. His own brother's word won't be questioned."

"You're forgetting the girl."

"Hardly," Reed murmured.

Claiborne stared at him for a full five seconds of disbelief. "You're willing to . . . your own niece?"

Reed said smilingly, "I'm an adaptable fellow. I've had to re-cast my life before this, adapt quickly to new circumstances. Necessities of survival."

Claiborne was baffled. Reed's easy, cold-blooded suggestions rang somehow true to character. Yet it was unbelievable that this man, reputed as a shiftless, gutless fop, should suddenly array himself in different colors.

Claiborne wondered whether the change was a ruse, whether Reed was merely biding his time through the immediate danger till he could see justice done his brother's killer.

Seeing the doubt harden in his face, Reed swiftly leaned forward across the table, the lamp flickering over his fleshy, pale features. "Claiborne. In the early part of the war, when your forces in the Tennessee border fighting were hard-pressed, you received help from a guerrilla band—Tierney's Raiders. They raided more than one enemy supply train to bring you food and ammunition."

"Yes," Claiborne growled, "for a price—the damned blackguards. Don't tell me you were with Tierney?"

"You met their leader face to face several times," Reed said impatiently. "Look at my face—carefully. Come on, man; it hasn't changed that much—"

"Cushing Tierney!" It left Claiborne in an explosive whisper.

Reed nodded and began to talk, quietly and quickly. Inside of five minutes Claiborne understood, but still he was puzzled.

"That's a dangerous secret," he said slowly, "very dangerous to entrust to anyone. Why tell me—Tierney?"

Reed spread his soft hands. "To show my good faith, to show we're birds of one feather. We can trust each other—" he smiled thinly— "to an identical limit."

Claiborne said narrowly, "Go on."

"Listen. I once saw the colonel's will. He left everything to his daughter. Cissie as good as told me in her fresh young way that when she inherited Lionclaw my presence here would no longer be tolerated. *She* made her mother no promise to shield her blacksheep uncle. The colonel's death plainly puts me out in the cold. Unless—" He paused, weighing the obvious.

"Unless," Claiborne said gently, "there were no Cissie?"

"Then," Reed said, "I'd be the only surviving member of the colonel's immediate family. No one to worry about but a few shirttail relatives back in Kentucky whose claims wouldn't hold water . . . especially should we forge a new will. The colonel's present will is locked in the safe in his room."

Claiborne understood now. "We can use each other, eh? Let it be known that you, the colonel's only heir, and I, holding the Armijo grant, agreed on an amicable settlement—share and share alike. Sparing both costly litigation and a too-close scrutiny by others of this whole affair. . . ."

Reed chuckled. "And how the colonel actually died need not go beyond this ranch. If your man Blaize will keep his mouth shut?"

"He will, for the right sum. What about the Lionclaw crew?"

"I'll pay them off in the morning—tell them to drift. They'll scatter far and wide, glad to get out with whole skins. The entire matter contains elements of chance, but the stakes are worth the risk."

"That brings us," Claiborne said heavily, "back to the girl." He paused to isolate his next words, said flatly, "I want no part of woman-killing."

"Squeamish, General?"

"No—sensible; that part's dynamite."

"Leave it to me," Reed said calmly.

"It'll have to be—an accident."

"Leave it to me," Reed repeated. "There's one more thing you probably don't know. . . ." He explained about Virginia Gilchrist's old Spanish charter, how it had passed into the hands of "Red John" Sykes, alias Charles McVey, how Sykes had offered to sell it to him.

Claiborne stroked his great beard a thoughtful moment. "Could this Gilchrist woman and her charter be a fake?"

"The colonel thought so. So did I, until McVey told me he'd verified its authenticity with an old fellow who was a servant in the Rivera family's household. This old Mexican's word is said to be infallible. That's one thing we can be sure of. The other is that this document is dangerous to us."

Claiborne nodded, his gaunt face sober. "After acquiring the Armijo grant, I did a good deal of research on judgments of rival property claims. The New Mexico courts have often decided in favor of the old Spanish grants. This one could supercede both our claims. But it will be useless to anyone except the Gilchrist woman. If it gets back into her hands—"

"We have to see that doesn't happen," Reed said flatly. "Sykes has the charter. We have to catch up with him before Owen Rutledge does."

They talked it over a while, Bloody Matt agreeing that after Reed had gotten rid of the crew, he and his men would go after Sykes alias McVey, while Reed handled the problem of his niece.

As they talked, there came a soft tramp of bootsteps on the back porch. Claiborne barely glanced up as the door opened, expecting to see Blaize. His restless eyes caught and froze on the man in the doorway—a huge man bulking larger in travel-stained clothes, a leveled gun in his fist.

ELEVEN

Searching the dead McVey's pockets, Owen had found an empty gambler's pistol, a canvas bag containing forty gold double-eagles, and a thin, oilcloth-wrapped packet. Removing the oilcloth, he guessed at first glimpse of the faded parchment what it contained. Kneeling in the flickering glow of Bayliss' lantern, he'd carefully spread out and examined the Rivera charter, afterward returning it to the oilcloth and tucking it inside a deep pocket of his sheepskin. He wondered tiredly how happy Virginia Gilchrist would be for its return . . . after she had heard everything. *You killed her man; no woman could help but hate you even after she knows the truth.*

The thought clung and nagged through a dragging weariness of mind and body as he helped Bayliss dig a shallow grave in the old camp cemetery back of the stable. When they had covered the blanket-wrapped body, he went up to his room and collapsed across the sagging cot without removing his coat.

Owen slept the deep, dreamless sleep of exhaustion. When he woke, the sun was high above Sunfire's ramshackle rooftops. He went down to the kitchen where Bayliss' wife heated some leftover steak and potatoes. Afterward he went to the stable. He saddled his bay and then out of curiosity went to where McVey's buckskin was stalled. Puzzled, he studied the Lionclaw brand on its hip. Cissie M'Kandless had said that McVey had not showed at Lionclaw; then McVey must have come in secret to Reed M'Kandless, forced him to turn over a fresh horse and probably the sack of money.

In fifteen minutes Owen was on the downgrade trail to Blanco Basin, leading the buckskin. He had no doubt of his immediate destination: Lionclaw. If Colonel M'-Kandless had shielded his brother-in-law Cushing Tierney while half-deceived as to Tierney's real character, this horse, the money, the charter, and a brief explanation should convince the colonel that Tierney had abetted the escape of an unmistakable thief and murderer. Owen considered, *If he won't turn Tierney over to the federals, you always can.* And hated the thought, hard face becoming iron-set. Tierney was his. He'd have him if. . . . For a detached moment he knew strong self-revulsion. This was what he'd become: little better than Tierney or Sykes or even Matthew Claiborne; men who used death and violence to selfish ends. *All right, don't think about it, shut it off. . . .*

He rode steadily through the rising heat of mid-day, chewing some hardtack and washing it down from his canteen without leaving the saddle. The shadows had lengthened across Lionclaw's immense, rolling grass flats. He rode steadily through the twilight and deep into the darkness, guided by the sawtoothed landmarks of basin-rimming peaks which he'd mentally charted on his first visit to Lionclaw headquarters. A moon-washed sky clearly etched the surrounding country.

Shortly after midnight he saw the black-blocked outbuildings ahead, and he came directly up on the rear of the hay shed. There he dismounted in the cottonwood grove and sidled along the building's flank to a front corner. A light showed from the bunkhouse fifty yards away. Late hours for a working ranch. . . . It added a puzzled note to his mounting apprehension about his reception here.

He was about to step from the shadows to cross the yard when the bunkhouse door opened. A man stepped out, paused in the lamplight to say something jocular over his shoulder, and then lounged across the yard, halting by the shed less than a dozen feet from Owen. He paused to urinate, grunted his relief, and took tobacco and papers from his shirt pocket. He shaped a cigarette leisurely, and Owen leaned forward to see his face in the flare of lamplight. A lean and wolfish face, strange to him. Yet he couldn't be sure he'd seen every Lionclaw crewman.

"Hey," Owen called softly. The man dropped his quirly in his haste to wheel around, claw back his coat. "No gun," Owen warned sharply as he stepped out to the moonlight.

The man said tensely, "Who the hell are you?"

"Man who wants to see the colonel without getting shot for a prowler . . . all right with you?"

The man laughed nervously. "That's all right with me. I'll take you to him."

He swung about as though to lead the way to the house; Owen saw his hand again dip slyly, unobtrusively, beneath the coat. Owen slipped out his Navy gun and took two long strides. The man wheeled, bringing out his gun, jaw falling slack as he saw Owen almost on him. Owen swung his pistol in a brief, savage arc that ended above the man's left ear. With a smothered sigh, he slumped forward and Owen caught him and dragged him inside the hayshed, letting him down in the shadows.

He paused in the doorway, narrowly studying the

lighted buildings. He could only guess blindly at the situation here . . . one way to learn the truth. He went across
the yard with a low-running stride and circled the main
house. Only the kitchen was lighted. He loped onto the
back porch and carefully opened the door, gun palmed
and cocked.

Matthew Claiborne's casual lifting glance found him
and froze to no expression at all. Owen stepped inside,
closed the door, and scooped Claiborne's pistol from the
table. He let it off-cock and shoved it into his belt, his
circling gaze hardening on the pasty, staring face of Reed
M'Kandless.

"General, I will give you five seconds to tell what's
happened here," Owen said distinctly. "Then I start
shooting."

Claiborne carefully lifted his hand and drew on the
cheroot. "I'd call you abrupt, Rutledge, not impulsive."
His glance warily fell to the Navy gun. "Steady down
now. I've met the enemy, they're mine. That should be
evident—"

"The colonel, his daughter?" Owen grated. "Speak up,
damn you."

Claiborne drew an unsettled breath. "Steady down,"
he repeated. "The colonel is dead. Heart attack, I didn't
kill him."

"Except indirectly. Cissie . . ."

"In her room, unharmed," Claiborne said jerkily. "Listen, I have four men in the bunkhouse. Guarding the
crew. One shot, you'll have them on your back."

Owen ignored him, hard glance slanting again to Reed.
Color drained slowly back to the stout man's face where
Owen saw the sly, fearful knowledge that Owen had
learned his identity. But the ruthless, raw courage that
had been Cushing Tierney's held the pale eyes steady
now.

Reed said softly: "You caught up with McVey—of
course?"

Owen was wordless, his grim stare unchanging. Reed
stirred uneasily. "Of course," he murmured, as if to himself.

"He lived long enough to talk, Tierney."

"And you'll kill me, I suppose." Reed shrugged, his round shoulders bracing stiffly beneath his quilted robe. "Well. . . ."

Owen drew Claiborne's gun from his belt, laid it on the edge of the table by Reed's arm.

"My men, Rutledge," Claiborne said softly.

Owen's grim glance shifted. "When they come, you'll be my life insurance." He looked back at Reed, waiting.

Reed's eyes lifted from the gun on the table. He did not stir a muscle. His lips barely moved. "I won't go for it, Rutledge. You've dogged me this far; don't let that stop you."

Owen sheathed his own gun. A nerve-strung stillness threaded away, broken by Claiborne's harsh intake of breath. Reed did not move, did not take his eyes from Owen's face. The ghost of a grin touched his thin lips.

Owen realized that his own body was trembling. *You bastard, you rotten smirking bastard, you know I won't, not this way.* He moved forward, towering above Reed with his great fist closing. He smashed it across Reed's jaw with a savage backhanded blow that toppled the heavy man's chair sideways. Reed fell face down and lay motionless.

"Yes, Rutledge," Matthew Claiborne said, "I'd call you abrupt—in your soft-hearted way."

Owen said wickedly, "Don't be premature, friend. Next time we meet he'll hold a gun if I have to strap it in his hand. This isn't the time. On your feet."

Claiborne didn't move. He said musingly, "If you caught McVey, you must have that very valuable Rivera charter now—eh?" Owen's silence seemed to satisfy him; he smiled. "Don't be an utter fool. We can make a deal. . . ."

Owen picked up the gun on the table and came close to Claiborne. He muzzled it against Claiborne's neck, thumbed back the hammer. "You can leave here one of two ways. Bloody Matt Claiborne should know when a man means it."

Claiborne inhaled slowly, slowly sighed out the breath. ". . . . All right." He placed his palms on the table and shoved to his feet, moved to the door ahead of Owen.

They crossed the moonlit yard at a fast trot, Owen shoving Claiborne ahead and glancing over his shoulder at the bunkhouse. Within moments Claiborne's men would be wondering why their comrade hadn't returned. As they passed the open-sided hayshed, a deep groan came from its darkness.

Claiborne halted. "What's that?"

"Buffaloed one of your poodles, he'll be coming to." Owen drove the pistol hard into Claiborne's ribs. "Get a move on."

They skirted the shed, plowed through its flanking brush into the dark cottonwoods. Owen saw his bay and the buckskin in the moon-dappled glade where he'd tethered them. "Hold it."

Claiborne's great height stiffened, but he stopped dead. Owen swung his gun up and down. Claiborne's hat muffled the blow and he sank heavily. Owen ran to the bay, caught the reins, toed into stirrup and swung up. As he careened the animal through the trees, he heard Bloody Matt's sudden-lifted bawl: "I'll ride you down, Rutledge! By God, I'll—"

Owen twisted in his saddle, shot into the trees. He heard Claiborne's shrill curse, the thrashing of brush as he retreated. Owen felt a bitter inward sinking as he spurred out of the trees and north across the flats. Claiborne's hat had blunted the blow enough to dangerously narrow the safe lead Owen might have had. In minutes they'd be on his trail—unless the necessity of holding the Lionclaw crew delayed them.

But Claiborne had known about the charter. Reed must have told him. That meant the two of them had joined forces, had been reciprocally scheming even as he'd had burst in on them. They had a strong incentive to drop everything and run him down. Owen squeezed the bay to a reckless run, heading for the far foothills to the north.

And slowly he became aware of a fresh danger—the bay's flanks were heaving, it was missing stride. The animal had been ridden for weeks with little rest. He had pushed it at a savage pace in his pursuit of McVey; the sturdy beast was reaching the limit of endurance. *Should have taken the buckskin,* he thought now, too late.

For the next two miles he held the animal in, finally halting on a vast stretch of night-silvered grass. The bay needed a few hours' stop, and he had to hone his thoughts to fresh decision. He threw off saddle and gear, hobbled the bay, spread his ground sheet and sat down, his knees drawn up. He took a stubby blackened briar from his sheepskin, and dug out the hard dottle with his pocket knife. It was the poorly kept pipe of a man who rarely smoked, except when alone with his thoughts. Now he merely put it between his teeth and absently sucked the stem.

Shortly at least five men would be after him on a blood hunt. He did not know the country or its people; there was nobody, no sanctuary, he could turn to. He could keep riding on, across the peaks, gain the safety of distance from Blanco Basin. But Virginia Gilchrist wanted her charter returned, and he wanted Cushing Tierney. He thought, too, of Cissie M'Kandless, alone back there with Claiborne and a treacherous uncle, though for the present she was safer there than she'd be had he taken her away. Any of these things was sufficient to hold him.

Owen squinted at the foothills, still distant across Lionclaw's great acreage. He would have to hole up, evade Claiborne's men till they quit the search. That might consume days, days for which he wasn't properly provisioned. *Jerky and hardtack'll have to stretch,* he thought stoically and settled his chin on his knees, sitting bolt upright so as to easily spot the first sign of pursuit on this open plain.

He nodded off several times through the hours that followed, but restless tension kept him jerking awake. When the first pink belt of dawn tinged the horizon, he rose, stiffly cramped, and unhobbled his horse.

Full dawn found Owen close to the foothills, holding the bay to a controlled pace. Soon he'd be deep in wild, irregular backcountry, with a wide choice of places to lie low. *But one good tracker in Bloody Matt's outfit can make it rough,* he worried, glancing continually over his backtrail. He shucked out of his sheepskin against the lifting heat, tied it behind his cantle.

Then his far-ranging stare picked out the distant specks that were horsemen. *They're coming fast, they've likely got that tracker, fresh horses, too.* He assayed these facts, added to them the miles remaining to the first foothills, totaled them to nothing good. Yet he resumed his held-in pace. The last thing he could afford was to founder the bay and put himself afoot against mounted men.

The land began to tilt upward, but still rolled out flat as a griddle. In a half-hour he paused to rest the bay. The riders were nearer now, coming on a straightaway course that told Owen he was long-seen. They were closing the margin fast. He shook his head, went on. Soon he rode into a deep cleft between the first shallow lift of hills, there struck the grass-grown ruts of an ancient logging road. It wound up a right-hand slope into tall pine timber. The sooner he penetrated good cover, the better; Owen followed the road.

Coming out on the crest of the wooded rise, he found that it dropped sharply away down a rocky, treeless slope. The road twisted sinuously down over a rotted corduroy base, and beyond lay a maze of gentle hills mantled by meadows interspersed with timber belts. The allover view was too open to suit, but he could not turn back now. He'd have to trust blind luck to take him through. Owen put the bay down the slope and cut northwest in a straight line that he hoped would give him a brief lead. The country was at least rugged enough to give the fresh mounts of the pursuit no advantage; they'd be held to roughly his pace.

He pulled up in the first jag of timber and surveyed his rear. No sign yet . . . he'd know shortly how good their tracker was. Owen crossed several more humpy pastures with their wooded skirmish lines and then topped an abrupt rocky ridge and saw beyond where the mean country began. It looked broken and cruel, studded with monolithic boulders and laced by treacherous slides. But the honeycombing of gorges and deep washes looked promising . . . a man should lose himself there. He looked back, saw the five riders just emerging onto the first meadow.

They were moving swiftly, spreading wide into a ragged line to beat through the timbered places. Then he caught a distant shout, saw them converge back to a bunch and come on. Knowing he was spotted, Owen savagely berated himself for not moving faster.

He nudged the bay down the ridge slope which sheered so steeply toward the bottom that the animal skidded the last few yards on its haunches in an avalanche of dislodged rubble. Owen kicked it up into the nearest canyon and rode steadily for a quarter hour, holding to the main trunk of the gorge against a hunted man's instinct to turn into the first small branch canyon, many of which cross-hatched the high walls. The pursuers would have to pause at each off-stem to make certain he hadn't turned in. Small delays . . . but every minute was precious now.

Then he swung around a bend and came to a dead stop. He faced a freak limestone ridge that ran to either side far as a man could see, with a vertical wall that reared skyward for a good three hundred feet. The gorge ran solidly against the wall and ended. Owen knew a sinking despair, threaded by fresh hope as he came close enough to see a trail—partly faulted out by geological convulsion, partly hand-chipped painstakingly by people of a forgotten age. It followed the facerock sideways at a comfortable angle to the summit . . . wide enough, he judged, to accommodate a single horseman.

He put the bay up the trail, picking out each hoofhold on a tight rein to which the horse responded well. The trail was literally scored into the rock with a hall-like overhang a bare foot above Owen's head; he couldn't tell what lay more than a few yards ahead. Ancient the trail might be, but still firm, and soon he breathed easily, steadily climbing.

Then he felt a constriction of panic as the ledge began

to narrow down. God . . . what a place to get trapped. He halted, his palms sweaty on the reins, leaning as far as he dared from the saddle. He made the mistake of glancing into the dizzy abyss below, and was careful not to look again. As much as he could see of the trail indicated that it did not quite pinch off, and afterward it widened again. *This'll be ticklish, but you can pass it.*

Owen dismounted and led the bay along the narrowing ledge. Part of the liprock had fallen away; this section of ledge, running perhaps a half-dozen yards, was rotted and crumbling beneath his boots. Again he halted. Here was the worst place. A man afoot would cross it cautiously; a horse's barrel would find it dangerously snug.

Owen flexed his clammy hands, spoke gently to the bay as he edged sideways hugging the cliff. The bay's flank scraped against the rock. One hoof slipped on the rounded ledge lip, sending a rattle of pebbles into the gulf. It stopped with a convulsive tremor of muscles. Owen tugged the reins, talking quietly. The bay came on. The footing widened solidly, and they were safely across.

Owen stood by the bay's head, rubbing its trembling shoulder. "Think you're the only one?" he murmured. Aware of the pressing delay, he mounted and headed up the last hundred feet. He came out on the rimrock and drew a deep breath of relief, seeing the gentle fallaway of the land beyond.

And now again the pursuers were close, turning out of the gorge mouth below. Owen heard their approach before he saw them and he led the bay back from the cliff and threw reins. His face tight, he worked along the rim to a point where the trail below shouldered well out from beneath its protective overhang. Numerous sizable boulders littered the rim. He chose one that was roughly block-shaped and knee-high, tested its weight with his shoulder. It was lodged solidly. He stooped and got his fingers beneath a crevice, braced his great shoulders and heaved. The boulder tilted on edge, grated over to lay poised on the rim.

He rested his hands against it, waiting. The riders

were mounting the trail. He heard voices, the creak of gear, the nearing clatter of iron on rock. He could not see them yet for the overhang. When the drift of noise grew directly beneath, he looked down and saw the first rider draw into view on the bare shoulder.

He gripped the block, lifted—so suddenly that its mass tumbled outward, he lost balance and had to scramble back. He heard it strike; a horse screamed and plunged off the ledge; the thin, wailing cry of its rider died away into the gulf. The boulder made a falling crash that drowned all other sound—a thinning rattle of gravel, silence.

Owen saw none of it. Sweating and shaking, he stood and bawled down, *"Keep your distance, you bastards!"* There was no reply, only a faint murmur of talk and more silence. They would not dare come on for a while.

Owen returned to his horse, gigged it into a trot down the far slope. Memory of the falling man's cry knotted around his guts. *He asked for it, they all did.* They'd hunted him like a beast, now they were cut to four. And Owen could think, *They asked for it,* feeling no better for the thought.

TWELVE

Owen sensed that he'd neatly boxed himself before the fact was confirmed.

A brief scare and the loss of a man would not hold Claiborne long, he'd known after leaving the cliff. Darkness was not many hours away; then he could move on while Clairborne's tracker was held to a standstill, leisurely lose himself on a trail where even an Indian would be baffled. More deep canyons lay beyond the cliff, but all dropped away sharply with no paths down.

He rode along the rim of one for several miles before finding a broken wall slide that formed a ramp to its base. It was a good six hundred feet to the bottom, and afterward the sheer walls held for many miles. Owen had no choice but to follow the twisting canyon floor.

It was thus that he came abruptly into a wide cove, a tiny grassed and wooded valley, around all sides of which, so far as he could tell, rose insurmountable walls.

To turn back to the slide area would cut it too fine; Clairborne's men must be nearly there. Unless he could find an exit here, he'd have to make a last-ditch stand.

Owen began a slow circuit of the walls, pushing the bay through deep brush, hoping for a chance fissure or tunnel concealed by overgrowth. Then he smelled wood-smoke, pungent on a shifting breeze.

Someone living here? he thought unbelievingly. Perhaps a maverick Indian . . . or a man hunted like himself. Owen slipped his gun from its holster and pushed on, skirting masses of fallen rock and rotted deadfalls, ramming the bay through tangles of vine-grown brush. He caught the smoke-smell now and again, each time stronger. Then he rounded a boulder the size of a small house and came on the camp.

The fire was smoking badly, evidently untended. The camper had picked out his approach some time ago, and was back in hiding—watching. *And with a ready gun; go easy,* Owen thought. Making no sudden move he sheathed his pistol and rode into camp with reins held at chest-level, hands in unmistakable view. A sizzling frying pan and steaming coffeepot were propped on stones close by the fire. Owen swung down and stood away from his horse.

"Grub's burning," he said quietly, clearly.

He did not turn immediately as boots scraped over rocks somewhere behind him. Then he did swing slowly on his heel. Missou Holbrook came at a light trot around the great boulder, rifle slacked loosely in the crotch of his arm.

"Man can't get off by himself nowheres," Missou murmured, walking to the fire. But a near-cheerful note to it let Owen guess how thin his own company had begun to wear. He laid his rifle down, wrapped a rag around his fist and lifted the frypan and coffee pot away from the fire, setting both on a low slab of rock. Owen tramped over and squatted down by him. Missou poured a tin cup of coffee which he silently extended. Owen accepted it, aware of a belly-knotting hunger; he grimaced, swore softly as he scalded his tongue.

Missou smiled faintly. "Take it easy, dig in." He speared a strip of sizzling bacon on his Barlow knife.

"No time." Owen set down the cup, his eyes fixing the slim youth. "There's a bunch set to nail my hide, coming fast. If you know a way out of this box, better tell it now."

Missou slowly lowered the bacon, frowning. "Only way out's way you came in. Who's coming fast?"

"Major Claiborne, three others."

"After you?"

"No time to tell it," Owen said flatly. "You lay low— keep out of sight when they come. Don't buy in."

Missou's smile broadened. "Won't be happy about taking on two, will they? Relax, grub up." Seeing the exasperated impatience on Owen's face, he added, "I heard your horse's iron hitting rocks when you were a half mile away. Canyon carries sound to beat all hell. You'll hear 'em plenty of time. . . . Those there fish are good."

Owen's glance fell to the skillet. "Fish?" He still wondered at Missou's half-calm, half-eager acceptance of the situation; the kid was likely champing at the bit with inactivity and solitude . . . and ready, so he guessed, to tackle wolves barehanded.

"Brook trout, sure. There's a stream rushes under the walls, full of 'em. I use shirt ravelings, a bent pin, some fat grubs. Fifteen minutes, I got my supper."

Owen wrapped a strip of bacon around a chunk of trout, began to eat—and found himself devouring ravenously. His appetite was scarcely blunted by the savory morsel. But Missou gave a faint, smiling nod at the food, sat back on his haunches to build a cigarette while

Owen cleaned up the skillet. He mopped up the last of the grease with a cold sourdough biscuit, swallowed it. He looked up to see Missou watching him through a furl of smoke, his expression quizzical and musing and faintly bitter.

"Nice here," the boy said quietly.

Owen glanced around, at the dark-aisled pine groves, the late sun mellowing an old-gold patina along the cliff summit. A not-distant brook made its muted, musical gurgle, and the wind soughed murmurously through the pine tops. It stirred a primitive, timeless spell through a man, this wildness and silence and solitude.

"Yeah," he said. Knowing that wasn't all Missou meant to say.

"I had it nice before you came," the boy went on softly. "That hassle in Blanco mixed me up. Had to get away off from things, think it all out. I found this place. Nothing like it. A man can sort things out, place like this."

"Sure."

"You've sort of busted it up."

Owen sensed with sudden insight that the sullen discontent marring the boy's words rose from a deeper dissatisfaction. Missou Holbrook hadn't yet sorted matters out as neatly as he desired. *You can't pigeonhole life, in your mind, you have to learn by living,* he wanted to tell the boy, but aloud he said only: "Sorry."

Missou's quick grin flashed. "Hell, don't matter. Time gets heavy on a man's hands here. I was cravin' a little excitement, you sure as all hell brought it. . . . Figured you and Claiborne would tangle again, after that hassle. What's it all about?"

Very briefly Owen told him. Missou was silent afterward, looking at the dead cigarette between his fingers, not seeing it. He said at last: "Sorry. About your friend. That big—Negro."

Owen said nothing, and then Missou spoke hesitantly: "Got underholts on a real wildcat, ain't you?"

Owen said quietly: "What I said before stands. When

the shooting starts, you lay low back in this brush. They'll never see you. . . ."

Missou was already shaking his head. "Why?" Owen demanded angrily. "My fight, mine alone. You admit you got some long living to sort out. Why throw it away to side someone you hardly know?"

That flashing grin again. "Four of them, two of us. About even odds, good chance we both live through. There's food here, berries, fish, clear water. Two men could hole up against an army, one standin' guard at the canyon mouth while the other sleeps, fixes grub, so on."

Owen nodded, unsmiling and patient. "That doesn't answer the question."

Missou flung his cigarette into the fire with a swift, irritated gesture. "Damn it, I took a liking to you. Want to question that, too?"

"No," Owen said, now smiling a little. "But you're feeling raunchy, too; you want to take a crack at something. Or someone."

"All right," Missou snapped, and then he laughed shortly. "All right, but I meant what I said." He looked into the fire a moment, arms folded on his knees. Owen watched the young face shift mood, a return of that musing bitterness. *How can a man get through to him?* Owen wondered, knowing that he could tell the kid nothing that Missou was not ready to hear, to learn for himself.

And then Missou opened the way, beginning to talk, hesitantly at first, but soon eagerly, spilling the rush of bitter memories. From this Owen pieced the riddle of the boy—his disillusionment, his easy fearlessness, his search for a goal worth a man's loyalty. The war had taken Missou's father and four brothers; and his mother, bearing too much grief, had died soon afterward. Missou was only thirteen when Appomattox came, and afterward had drifted around the homes of his shirttail relatives, who happened to include the infamous clans of the Daltons, the Youngers, the Jameses.

Though they'd ridden with Quantrill's butchers and were outlawed by a hated Union, the James boys were protected as modern Robin Hoods by the people of their native Clay County. Young Holbrook, glowing with hero worship, had spent his adolesdence hobnobbing with Frank and Jesse and Cole Younger in their own households. The gradual realization that his heroes were common thieves and murderers was the second crushing blow in his vulnerable youth.

Desperately seeking anew, he'd followed the great American dream that was moving westward, and found only a brawling, dog-eat-dog frontier. And Owen understood the unspoken yearnings for something better behind the search that had hardened a sensitive boy into a conviction that only top dogs like Ivy North won a violence-pocked place in the frontier jungle. These were the ones to follow and emulate. Only, the shiny-eyed streak of boyhood he'd never lost had suddenly caviled at the murder of an old man. On this pivot of decision Missou had rebelled. *But easy as not he could slip back,* Owen thought. *Unless.*

As Missou sat then in a shamed, angry silence, plainly feeling he'd said too much, Owen prodded mildly: "So you came here to think things over."

"Why not? It's peaceful here, clean, no dirty damned people. Should have thought of this before."

Owen said immediately, flatly, "It's selfish."

"What?"

"You can't stay here forever. Be nice if a man could wall himself off . . . from all that out there. But he can't. Sooner or later he has to go back."

"Damn fine thing if he didn't have to, though!"

"No. It's selfish. And it's wrong. Fine for a man to get off by himself sometimes, one thing a man can't do around other people is think clear. But a man always has to go back. Because he's part of it, boy, part of the human race. The whole brawling slew of it, good or bad. And if he doesn't find a meaning, a reason, then he's got to make one for himself. Otherwise . . ." Owen hesitated . . . "he's a damned vegetable, rooted in his own muck."

"Know it all, don't you?"

"Damned little. I try to learn . . . a few things."

"Then you tell me where," Missou said savagely, "I can find a few reasons. Even one."

"I'll give you two," Owen said steadily. "Two women who need help. And nobody to help them but us. If you're willing to try."

Missou toyed with a twig, snapped it in two, frowning. "You mean this Eastern lady you was talking about, Miss Gilchrist—and Colonel M'Kandless' girl?"

"If you're willing to try," Owen repeated, very slowly. "This is no job for a wet-eared, thrill-seeking kid. Nothing to be gained except maybe a bullet. Maybe something else, like growing up a little."

Missou watched him steadily, was about to speak. Owen lifted a quick hand—listening. He'd caught the distant, thin-echoed clank of iron on rock. . . .

Missou stood up, his rifle in hand. "Well," he said quietly, "you waiting for something?"

THIRTEEN

Massive chunks of rimrock had long crumbled from the surrounding heights and fallen to the cliff base. Owen and Missou took positions behind two of these just within the canyon where it debouched into the valley. Both had '66 Model Springfields in .50 caliber; they divided their cartridges evenly, lined them in convenient rows in rock niches, and waited, stationed on either side of the canyon mouth.

Missou said softly, "How we take 'em?"

"No killing."

Missou gave a low, wry whistle.

"You ever blood a man, kid?"

"Not yet. Bluffed a few."

"We can bluff here. Place your shots close, pin them down."

"This canyon runs pretty wide," Missou pointed out. "They could rush us all abreast."

"If it comes to that," Owen said wearily, and fell silent. If Claiborne led a mounted attack, there would be no choice: shoot to kill. *You've had enough of that, way too much.* The coming darkness might point a way out. Two of them could pin back the pursuers till then.

He could pick out plainly the sounds of Claiborne's approach. He set his rifle across the rock, bearing down on the gorge's first sharp bend. Claiborne and one of his riders swung into view, coming on easy. Owen glanced at Missou who nodded, waiting his cue. Owen laid his shot at the feet of Claiborne's mount. The pie-bald fiddlefooted, and Claiborne held him in, and then Missou's rifle roared, the slug flailing gravel against the other horse's legs. The animal reared as his rider fought for control. Owen was already thumbing a fresh load into his gunbreech, but Claiborne abruptly spun his mount back around the bend, and his rider followed.

A full minute passed; voices murmured consultation downcanyon. Then Claiborne's voice raised with an angry, harried note. "Rutledge? Rutledge, who you got there?"

"Six Apaches armed to the teeth," Owen called.

Claiborne gave a strained laugh. "I thought I saw his face . . . that kid who was with North?"

"And five Apaches."

Missou couldn't control a spasm of laughter. Claiborne cursed them both blisteringly. Missou grinned at Owen. "You got him going." The kid looked swiftly back at the bend as the blued muzzle of a rifle tilted warily around the rock. Missou took quick aim, waited till the man's eye lifted along the sights, and fired. Rock fragments showered the man's face and he dropped back with a howl.

They settled to a long, wary vigil. Through the hours that followed, as sunset muted the canyon walls to a pale blue, Claiborne made no move. After a long interval Missou stirred restlessly. "What's he waiting for?"

"Dark, same as us."

"You got an idea for then?"

"I don't know. See what happens."

"Kid!" Claiborne's hail came on the heel of Owen's words. "You, Holbrook. Don't be a young fool. No mix of yours. Ride out of here."

Missou winked at Owen, called soberly, "With how many bullets in my back?"

"I don't want you, damn it! Nor Rutledge for that matter, if he's sensible; what I want is that Rivera charter. Don't be damned altruistic fools!"

Missou and Owen exchanged grim glances, with the tacit common thought that Bloody Matt could not afford to let either of them live only to become hidden enemies somewhere at his back.

"We're not that foolish," Owen called.

"You've had your warning, Rutledge. Several warnings, in fact. And now your last!"

The sunset blurred into twilight. Owen took a packet of jerky from his saddlebag, removed a strip and tossed the rest across to his companion. As he methodically chewed the tough, fibrous beef to a pulp that would slide down his throat, he saw a low beginning flare of firelight from beyond the bend. His jaws stilled, watching the high-leaping glare band the broad canyon from wall to wall, wipe back the shadows that would conceal a trapped man's exit.

"That ties it," Missou whispered. "We don't slip out, they don't slip in."

Owen digested this, his mind running over the situation . . . Claiborne would doubtless name off guard shifts to keep an alert. Unless they proposed to settle into a dragged-out siege, there was one chance out, a thin one. And Owen, thinking of Cissie M'Kandless' scheming uncle and the girl's danger, knew they must not wait. Except till full darkness. . . . In a whisper he told Missou the plan, and the boy soberly agreed, trying unsuccessfully to hide his reckless delight at this calculated risk.

When night had sabled down the valley for several hours and Owen guessed that Claiborne's tired men would be sleeping except for the guard, he and Missou silently retreated to Missou's camp back in the trees. They worked a half-hour, cutting up their ground sheets into four square pieces each and their ropes into four equal lengths apiece. They folded each piece of tarp several times, lifted each of their horses' feet and tied the pieces securely around the hoof just below the hock.

When they'd finished, Owen straightened, turning to the boy. He saw Missou shiver, guessed that like himself the boy's body was tension-sweated beneath his clothes, then chilled by the bitter mountain night. But Missou murmured, "I'm freezing in my guts. I'm scared, really scared."

Owen felt a warmth toward the boy that his previous cold courage hadn't inspired. He squeezed Missou's wiry arm, hard. "Buck fever. Just follow me, hear?"

"I'm damn well not backing out!"

"I know that." Owen repacked his gear, cinched it behind the cantle, and swung on. He paced the stock-inged bay a few yards across a bare rock surface, was satisfied by the muffled hoof-falls, and then they moved slowly down the valley toward the canyon.

They picked their way at a whispered tread down the boulder-littered canyon floor. Owen, watching the fitful blaze wash the walls ahead, listened for telltale sound. There was none. He edged the bay around the bend, halted at the circle of firelight. Three blanketed forms surrounded the centered fire. The guard sat on a rock against one wall, head bent as he fashioned a cigarette. His rifle leaned between his knees.

Owen slammed in his spurs. The bay launched forward like a released arrow, into the space between the fire and the canyon flank opposite the guard. His face bent almost into the mane, Owen heard the guard's yell as he sped abreast of the fire and on past. Then the pain burst along his back—mingling with the report of the guard's rifle.

Owen reeled, knowing in one shocked instant that the

bullet had angled up into his shoulder muscles, that it was a bad hit. Then the crash of Missou's Colt, the guard's pained yell. Owen held leather with a concentrated desperation, guiding the bay at a dangerous unslackened run up the dark gorge. Missou pounded steadily in his lead . . . a drift of frenzied shouts from the camp behind.

A half-hour later the two of them were crouched between two sheltering slabs of rock beyond the canyon, after achieving its top rim from the slide trail. The waning moon shafted enough faint light between the rocks for Missour to examine Owen's wound and apply a hasty bandage of torn-up shirt. Sitting on the ground, Owen bent his head between his knees, sweated with still-searing pain, fighting off the black, dizzy waves that tided rhythmically against his mind with each breath.

He realized that Missou was shaking him by the shoulder. ". . . can't stay here, Owen. They won't track us farther'n the canyon bottom till come daylight. We got to find a safe place before then."

Owen dredged up a whisper. "Hole up . . . hold 'em off."

"No," Missou said sharply. "That's a bad hole, bullet angled in deep. It's got to be cut out, wound swabbed clean. I seen men die of infected ones. You need proper care, proper dressing."

"Town then . . . Blanco. . . ."

"Sure," Missou said anxiously. "But it's a long ways . . . have to ride all night, and no easy pace. Can you make it?"

"Can if you . . . tie me in saddle."

"But where to in Blanco? They'll be on our tail when it's light enough, they'll come fast. If we're lucky enough to beat 'em into Blanco . . . anyone there who'll hide you?"

Missou's words seemed unreal, echoed from a distant, closing fog. Owen nodded dreamily, whispering, "Why sure. . . ."

FOURTEEN

Virginia Gilchrist prepared a lonely breakfast in her little kitchen. Usually she enjoyed a pleasant daily ritual before school began, eating leisurely and reading for a half-hour over two cups of coffee. But this morning, as for the last two, she barely tasted her food, gulped the coffee quickly. It only gave her a dull heartburn, and she shivered, unwarmed, and drew her faded gray wrapper tighter around her shoulders. She looked at the cold food in her plate, grease-marbled now, and pushed it away in revulsion. Her head ached from sleeplessness. She leaned her elbow on the table, hand rubbing her closed eyes.

What's the matter with you? she asked silently, knowing the answer she was reluctant to admit. The story of Abner's killing by Charlie McVey had been all over town the next morning; the stable hostler, who'd witnessed it, had been able to add nothing to the mystery. *It's terrible, terrible,* Virginia thought . . . remembering the look on Owen Rutledge's face as he'd left her house. To find Charlie, of course.

She shuddered . . . Through the three days and nights that had followed, Virginia had worried out every cranny of her mind, seeing in bitter clarity the insulated self-centeredness of her own existence; realizing with a deep uneasiness that it was Owen Rutledge, not McVey, for whom she was worried. Of course she didn't want Charlie's blood on Owen's hands, though Charlie plainly merited punishment . . . but what if Owen, not McVey, were the one to die? This thought she hated to front most, yet it was most persistent, recurring through sleeping and sleepless fantasies. And with this fresh insight, she could concede the suppressed excitement she'd felt at their first meeting, which had lingered with her. Even McVey had hinted at it.

She felt lost, tired, and hopeless here in her cozy kitchen. Warm tears formed against her palm. *I don't care about the stupid charter. Let him come back alive. Please.*

The back door shook with a hard blow. She glanced up, startled. There was a second, violent beat of a hammered fist. She rose quickly and went over, shot back the bolt. The door was pushed roughly wide.

She saw Owen Rutledge, his head tilted on his chest, weight slumped against a thin-faced young man whose light blue eyes were marred with a harried impatience.

"Miss Gilchrist?"

"Yes . . . but—"

The youth pushed unceremoniously past, and nudging the door shut with his toe, almost unbalanced himself under his companion's weight. Owen was held erect by an involuntary bracing of his legs and an arm thrown around the youth's neck. Virginia saw that both were bearded and filthy, that Owen's clothes were stiff with dried blood; she felt a wave of palsied sickness and fought against it.

The boy, she realized, was speaking impatiently: "No time to lose, ma'am. There a doctor in Blanco?"

She nodded, unable to speak.

"You'll have to get him. Just now we need a place to lay Owen down."

Virginia felt an abrupt, sure calm—a relief from the corroding tension. Owen was here, hurt but alive, and she could help him. She nodded briskly, her tone crisp: "Bring him into my room."

She hurried ahead and opened a door off the parlor, circled the small, neatly made cot as the youth laid Owen's weight gently across it, face down. Virginia turned his head, arranged the pillow beneath it, and looked at the boy. "How did this happen?"

He removed his hat, drew his sleeve across his mouth, talked quickly. Virginia studied his young face, seeing it dark and strained, quietly capable without being hard.

Before he'd finished, Owen groaned softly. She told the boy to lift him a little, and she opened his coat and shirt. Her mouth tightened at what she saw—blood-caked bandages which hadn't halted the copious bleeding. They would have to be soaked off.

She looked up at the boy who was silent now, fidgeting with impatience. "Your name is—?"

"Missou Holbrook, ma'am."

"How did you happen to come here, Mr. Holbrook?"

"Had to bring Owen somewhere. Before passin' out he told me how to find your place . . . no place else he could go."

Virginia felt a quick glad warmth, concealed it coolly: "And you say Matthew Claiborne and his men are following you?"

"Yes'm. Had a good lead on 'em coming out of the foothills, while it was still dark. Owen like he is, it took me a good ten hours gettin' here. Claiborne and his boys would have been on our trail long before dawn. One of 'em's a middlin' fair tracker. Once he picked out our tracks cutting straight for town, they'd be comin' fast. No sign as I rode in, but they must be close. Thing is, will they know where to look?"

"They might make a good guess," Virginia said. "Didn't you say that Owen has my charter—that Claiborne wants it?"

"Yes'm. Beg pardon." Missou dipped into a pocket of Owen's sheepskin and handed the familiar oilcloth sheaf across the bed. She turned it meaninglessly in her hands, then laid it on the bedside stand. She looked up to meet Missou's curious, slightly cold gaze. "Hope it was worth it," he said quietly.

"Nearly at the cost of a good man's life, you mean?"

"Not my words, ma'am," Missou answered stiffly.

"But your meaning. You are right, Mr. Holbrook. And what's to be done now?"

She saw his mood shift grimly on the youthful face. "Now we see to keeping him alive. When Claiborne comes, he'll likely force his way into your house. Unless . . ."

"Unless?"

"Maybe I can lead him off." Missou paused, carefully weighing this. "I'll need a fresh horse. Mine's tuckered, Owen's is almost dead on its feet. I left 'em out back. I'll take 'em to the livery, rent a nag, and wait where I can spot Claiborne when he rides in. I'll ride out where he can see me, cut the dust like I was just leaving town, and ran into him by chance. If they think I got your paper, they'll try ridin' me down."

"But—if they don't?"

Missou thought again, rattled swift directions. Together they eased Owen's inert weight off the bed onto the rug beside it. Missou tugged the low cot over his body. "Providin' they don't give a close look, that should hide him."

Wordlessly Virginia pointed at bloodstains on the wrinkled counterpane. Missou threw back the bedclothes and mussed the sheets and pillow. "When they come, they rouse you out of bed, see. . . . What's your work, ma'am?"

"Why, teaching school."

"You were sick today, stayed abed."

She nodded. "You had better hurry, Mr. Holbrook."

She followed him to the kitchen, where he paused to glance at the soiled breakfast dishes. "I'll hide them," Virginia said. "Please hurry . . . take care."

His face warmed with a heat-lightning grin. "Don't you fret, I'll lose them in short order. I'll come back tonight; we'll figure what's to be done."

"Yes, do that."

His smile thinned, and he was plainly troubled. "Sorry I brought you into this. They're mean-dangerous, playing for keeps. Can't be sure they'd not harm a woman. . . ."

"You did what had to be done. I'll be all right. Hurry now."

After he was gone, Virginia shoved the dishes out of sight in a cupboard and returned to the bedroom. She bent to look at Owen . . . eyes closed in his pale, close-bearded face; breathing noisily through his open mouth. Her heart pounded fearfully . . . he needed medical attention. But she couldn't risk going for Dr. Hart until Claiborne had made his appearance . . . and left.

She fetched a basin of hot water, and some clean cloths, pulled the cot from above Owen and set to soaking away his bandages. Virginia removed the bloody tatters, cleansed the wound as best she could. Fresh blood welled at once from the ugly hole, but now that he was still, the bleeding had lessened. She made a clean compress and affixed it with long strips tied around his chest. As she fumbled with the last knot, she heard commotion in the street . . . a body of horsemen thundering by.

Virginia lifted the cot back into place, shoved the basin and dirty bandages beneath it. She ran from the bedroom and through the parlor. She opened the front door a crack and strained her eyes down the dust-moiled street. Claiborne and his men had pulled up two blocks down. Beyond them a lone rider was heading from town. Missou Holbrook. Matthew Caliborne was nonplussed.

She saw his gaunt height swing in the saddle, his angry shouted orders carrying clearly: "Blaize, take Danny and search that small white house yonder, the Gilchrist woman lives there. Clay and I will go after Holbrook. If you don't find Rutledge or the charter, follow us."

Virginia closed the door and hurried back to her room. She sank onto the edge of her cot, heart pounding angrily. She bit her lip, forced her thoughts steady. Realizing that her hair was neatly arranged atop her head, she unpinned and let down the thick black braids. She thought: *This man Blaize . . . you've seen him on the street. He always tipped his hat, even bowed, though he didn't know you. He's a man a woman can handle.*

With this relieving thought came a soft, insistent tapping at the door. She rose, not too quickly, and went to answer it. Blaize stood hat in hand, a tall, yellow-haired man whose usually bleak eyes were shifting and uneasy; beside him was a barrel-shaped man who met her glance with a slack, arrogant grin.

Virginia gave them a wan, sleepy smile. "Yes?"

"Apologies, ma'am," Blaize muttered, "must ask you

to take us through your house. Looking for a man, believe he might have come here."

She opened the door wider. "This is quite irregular. This man . . . ?"

"You'll be knowin' him. Owen Rutledge."

"Certainly," she said evenly. "And do you think that I admitted him . . . in this state?" She drew the robe closer to her throat, giving him an outraged look.

Blaize reddened and stammered something. The man called Danny drawled amusedly, "Look, lady—"

Blaize's elbow drove viciously against his thick middle. Danny doubled with a wheeze of pain. "Take your hat off," Blaize snarled, and to Virginia with sharp impatience: "Ma'am, I must ask you to move aside. We're searching the house."

"I can hardly prevent you," she said coldly.

She followed them through the rooms. Hand on his gun, Blaize catfooted warily from parlor to kitchen. Danny rolled sullenly in his wake. The Texan's face bore a fixed, uneasy scowl, and he was careful not to look at her. Finally he halted in the doorway of her room.

Virginia stepped up beside him—and her breath constricted sharply. In plain sight on the bedside stand was the cloth-wrapped charter. Frozen, she watched Blaize's gaze idly touch different objects in the room. Trying to hide her desperation she asked, casually: "Aren't you Mr. Blaize?"

He looked at her with surprise. "Why, yes'm."

She smiled up at him. "I really don't have to ask. We've met before, and I was curious enough about your wonderful manners to learn your name." She frowned slightly. "You're certainly the last man I should expect to invade my home."

His dusty boots creaked with a shift of weight, his long face unhappier than ever. "See, this Rutledge fellow killed a man. Lawyer named McVey. We're part of a posse. Ain't inferrin'," he added hastily, "that you'd hide a killer, but it's said he was seen talkin' with you. We wounded him, he'll look to lay low. Could of come here, lied to you to get your help."

"I see," she nodded, covering a sharp, regretful pang at the revelation of McVey's death. "However I had heard that McVey murdered Mr. Rutledge's Negro friend. . . ."

"All the same, can't take law into his own hands that-away."

"Of course not," she said primly. "As to Mr. Rutledge's being seen with me, that is correct. I had hired him—for a small errand; that was the limit of our relations." She pressed her fingers to her temples. "I'm sorry; I don't feel well—"

Blaize studied her face mercilessly. "You ain't seen him since?"

"I have not," she lied proudly.

"For crissake," Danny began disgustedly. Blaize's soft tones razored off his speech. "You heard the lady, and we looked."

"There's a dozen places—"

"Danny."

The short man shrank from the unveiled warning in Blaize's look. He said no more. Virginia nodded demurely to the Texan's stumbled apology as she showed them to the door. When it closed behind them, she leaned against it a moment, knees weak and her body trembling wildly. When she had herself under control, she returned to the bedroom and hauled the bed away from Owen.

She'd noticed, with mingled fear and relief when Blaize approached the room, that the hurt man was utterly silent. Bending close now she saw with a flood of thankfulness that he was breathing quietly but evenly. The wound dressings were freshly stained, the bleeding not quite checked. *But Dr. Hart will have to probe for the bullet.*

She steeled her thoughts again, went to her small closet and opened it. She hesitated, feeling a warm flush along her veins as she glanced at the unconscious man. Angry at her shamed modesty, she moved the closet door ajar to cut her off from sight of him. *Mock maiden stupidity,* she berated herself coldly as she let the robe and night-gown slip to the floor.

Irresistibly she felt her eyes drawn to the tall tarnished

mirror above the commode across the room. *Too thin,* she thought critically, even as the reflection mocked her with a small ivory image slender and graceful as a New England birch, yet gentling into soft curves and hollows. She was aware of the man again, now with a hot, quickening excitement that was alien and frightening.

She dressed quickly and almost ran from the room. By the time she reached the street, walking prim and straight-backed toward the doctor's office, her expression was again an ivory-modeled coolness. But her thoughts were a disturbed tumult . . . her ideas of love were of a story-book variety, often read, never experienced. *What is this?* she wondered. *What's happening to me?*

FIFTEEN

Reed M'Kandless stood on the wide front veranda of Lionclaw's main house, one pudgy hand toying with the watchchain on his Marseilles-silken waistcoat, the other stroking his spade beard. His crafty eyes were troubled and faintly baffled.

He had not expected this afterwash of conscience when he'd casually suggested to Matthew Claiborne that his sister's daughter be put out of the way. He hadn't counted on the time-blurred memories that had swarmed back on him later, when he was alone and could fully consider this enormity to which he was now committed. He had remembered Cissie as a child, her chubby little arms circling his neck, or as a baby cooing and gurgling on his knee.

He'd told himself that those memories belonged to another place and time and world, when he was still an amiable young rakehell loafing off his family's bounty. A hundred things had since corroded a warm uncle-niece affection into a mutual, barely tolerating, dislike. Now the girl was only an obstacle to his greed, a danger to his security. Cushing Tierney, guerrilla, would have casually and ruthlessly crushed the irritant. But seven years of ease had softened Cushing Tierney in more than body; he shrank from the notion of arranging this murder that must appear accidental. If only he could personally avoid the sight and touch of her death . . . and then he thought he'd seen a way out.

Before Claiborne had left to run down Owen Rutledge, his men had ordered out the ranch crew at gunpoint with all their belongings—save for one man, Bob Fitz. Fitz's arm had been shattered by the bullet he'd taken resisting the invaders; that was adequate excuse to keep Fitz bedridden awhile. When Claiborne had gone, Reed had personally set Fitz's arm, left him with a bottle of whiskey for his pain.

Reed was not worried that the other crewmen might return. They would drift from the basin, workaday cowhands with no stomach for standing up to Claiborne's gunnies. Loyalty to the colonel might have held them, but the colonel was dead. Of a heart attack, they were told. The shot which had killed him was explained away as a warning slug Claiborne had fired over Reed's head. Only the segundo Paul Dirksen might offer a problem; he was not a man to run. But Dirksen had left with the others, his iron will holding him in the saddle, nursing a wounded side. Dirksen would be no trouble for at least a time.

That, Reed thought now, left Owen Rutledge and Claiborne himself. He'd hoped that Claiborne and Rutledge might kill each other in the ensuing chase. Both were potential dangers not merely to his plans but to his life. He shivered, remembering Rutledge's face; next time there would be no reprieve. As for his forced alliance with Claiborne, he'd as soon have bargained with the devil. In the ex-military careerist was a ruthless greed to match his own, and except for Cissie, Reed alone knew how Colonel M'Kandless had met his death.

Reed had also realized belatedly how Claiborne's counter-knowledge of his identity might be actually turned to a weapon in Claiborne's hands. Once they were safely partnered in secure ownership of Lionclaw, Claiborne's partner could be shot and his body turned over to the Territorial Marshal with Claiborne's claim that he'd uncovered the fact of Reed's true identity, had confronted him with it—and was forced to shoot.

Reed had considered it all carefully. Claiborne needed him alive a while yet—but he did not need Matthew Claiborne. Once rid of Claiborne, he must find and destroy both Virginia Gilchrist's Spanish charter and Claiborne's Mexican grant. Then his position was secured. Baldly stated, these objectives were simple. But there were a hundred complications in the doing. . . .

More than thirty hours had passed since Claiborne had pursued Owen Rutledge north from Lionclaw. One or both of them might be dead by now; Rutledge had had the Rivera charter; it might now be in Claiborne's possession. . . .

Reed shook his head. *Cross your bridges as they come,* he thought coldly. Just now there was Cissie. . . . If he handled Fitz properly, that problem was as good as eliminated.

He stepped off the veranda and walked down the gravel drive toward the bunkhouse. The early sunlight was warm and bright, the rich lawn still dew-sparkling. *A good time for someone to die,* he thought ironically.

Nearing the bunkhouse, he heard Cissie's low murmur within, then Fitz's angry, drink-slurred curse. "Gedadda here, you overgrowed witch!" Something hit the wall with a clatter.

Cissie came out, walking fast, her face an angry pink save where the ugly dark bruise left by Claiborne's fist mottled her jaw.

"What seems to be the trouble?" Reed asked mildly.

She threw out a hand helplessly. "I only wanted to make him comfortable. I spent fifteen minutes trying to reason with him. He was obviously in pain, but wouldn't let me touch him . . . then he threw a bottle at me."

"Perhaps I can make him listen."

"You?" There was faint contempt in her tone, and he knew she was thinking of how, as they had buried her father in the little cemetery plot by his wife, back of the house, he had counciled passive acceptance of their situation, saying that he'd try to dicker with Claiborne to prevent further violence. She'd passionately replied that since there were no men left on Lionclaw, she would shoot her father's murderer herself when he returned. *Which would solve part of my trouble nicely,* Reed thought now with sour amusement. Looking into her clear, angry hazel eyes, he knew another pang of regret, but a brief one.

"I can try. Prove I'm not wholly the foppish coward you think."

"Well," she said grudgingly, "be careful then. He has a gun, must have had it hidden beneath his bunk." Claiborne had appropriated all the crew's weapons. She ignored Reed's word of thanks, striding past him toward the house.

Reed stepped through the low doorway, and walked casually to Fitz's bunk. The small man was reclining with his head lifted, watching his visitor with bloodshot, pain-filled eyes. His pale bony torso was naked, gleaming with sweat, one arm splinted and fixed in a cloth sling. A heavy Colt lay across his belly.

"Goddamn it," he whispered viciously, "get me a doc, can't you!"

Reed squatted down, rocking back on his heels. "Your arm's fixed as good as any sawbones could do. I set a lot of broken limbs in the war. It's rough, eh, Fitz?"

"God, yes." Fitz's husky whisper was drunkenly slurred. "Got another bottle some'eres?"

"Might be another in the house, I'd have to look," Reed said idly. He was silent a moment, broaching this cautiously: "She bother you any?"

"That overgrowed witch!" The hateful edge returned to Fitz's tone. "She'd of liked to make like she was fussing over me whilst she schemed ways to make me hurt more . . . them big ones is all alike. Mean, rotten stinkin' mean. . . ."

"I know," Reed said sympathetically, but his smile was one of icy satisfaction. He'd noted long ago that Fitz was full of a stupid and lazy man's empty, half-hearted daydreams. Such a man could only fail at whatever he attempted. Over Fitz's life, frustration and failure had become rutted into a single bitter channel which was his excuse for self-failure: his unreasoning, savage hatred of larger people, men and women. Now, after two days of festering in a welter of whiskey and pain and self-pity, he'd be easy handling.

Reed drew a deep breath, plunged with a point-blank query: "Fitz, could you kill someone for a thousand dollars?"

Fitz's thin lips formed a wolfish grin. "Who you want dead that bad, mister?"

"Her. The girl. Cissie."

Fitz's jaw dropped slackly. "Jesus," he said softly. "You mean it, don't you?"

Reed talked very quietly and carefully, repeating himself over and over to etch how it must be done into Fitz's drunken brain. It had to look like an accident . . . and here was five hundred in advance. He drew a sheaf of bills from his pocket, money that he'd removed earlier from the colonel's safe.

"Damn," Fitz whispered, his eyes shining feverishly, eagerly. Then they dulled with a flicker of fear. "Woman-killin' . . . bad business."

Reed pressed it mercilessly. "I recall your bragging, in one of your sweet tempers, how you once knifed a big Mex girl down in Sonora."

"That bitch," Fitz muttered. "Laughed at me. A cheap crib whore. And she laughed at me . . . 'dirty little gringo with a face like a rat,' she called me!" His voice rose to an agonized frenzy.

"You'll never be anything but a little man, Fitz," Reed went on brutally. He slapped his hand across the Colt's as Fitz tried feebly to bring it up. "A little man trying to play a big one. That's if you continue to play it like a big man. But a man with money can be anything he wants. He can have the big girls crawling at his feet."

Reed's voice lowered to a hiss. "Think of that, Fitz . . . a thousand dollars at one time is more than you'll ever see as a thirty-and-found cownurse. Properly invested in a small ranch, a business, that thousand could carry you to anything you want to be. And handled as I told you, the girl's death will never be considered other than an unfortunate accident."

Fitz stared at him open-mouthed. If he was small on brain, he had more than his share of cocky ego. "Why sure," he whispered. "All I ever needed was a chance. Nobody never give me a decent chance. . . ."

A half-hour later Reed stood on the veranda, thumbs tucked in his waistcoat pockets, smiling his self-content as he watched Fitz and Cissie ride down the ranch road toward town. Fitz, he'd told Cissie, had regretted his behavior, and he had persuaded the little man to go to town and have Dr. Hart look at his arm. As Fitz was in a bad way, it would be kindly of Cissie to see that he made the nine-mile ride all right. Impressed by her uncle's tactful handling of the vicious little man, Cissie had readily agreed.

And that is the end of Cissie, Reed thought contentedly, watching the pair grow smaller on the long road . . . relieved that a dirty job had passed out of his hands. Of course sooner or later, in one of his drunken stupors, Fitz would brag how he'd been hired by Reed M'Kandless to murder his own niece. But Fitz must return to collect the balance of his pay; one bullet, and the body safely disposed of, would eradicate future danger. Nobody would think twice of the disappearance of a dirty, disagreeable little saddle tramp.

Reed turned his attention to the problem of Matthew Claiborne. He decided to wait here the rest of the day; if Claiborne hadn't appeared by then, he'd go into Blanco. Claiborne might have returned there for some reason. Once their leader was taken care of, his hired gunnies would not take up the fight.

SIXTEEN

When he spurred out of Blanco, Missou Holbrook had less than a hundred yard lead on Matthew Claiborne. Still he wasn't greatly worried. On a fresh livery mount, he should easily out-distance the pursuit.

He let his nag out at an easy lope, pacing them at first and holding to open country to lead them on. He looked back and saw only two riders in his wake. The other pair would be searching Virginia Gilchrist's house. Though he'd half-expected as much, swift uneasiness touched Missou; would their thin preparations fool Claiborne's toughs? Bloody Matt himself would not be easily misled. But Missou couldn't tell at this distance whether the leader was one of the pair on his trail.

To the north Missou saw a lift of broken formations, and he veered that way in an all-out run. The livery horse was an ugly jug-headed brute who fought the bit, but he was long-limbed, rangy and powerful. The mile-eating pace pulled them quickly near the broken area, which Missou now identified as a single formation composed of barren granite ridges, cut by winding gorges and littered with jumbled boulders. He headed up a narrow trail which brought him quickly to the crest of a ridge. He pulled in to scan his backtrail.

The two riders had not only fallen behind, but had pulled to a halt. The other two were coming from town at a hard gallop. They reached the waiting pair, merged into a brief, tight group to confer. Then all of them spurred on toward the ridges. An exuberant lift of relief drew Missou's quick grin. If they'd found Owen and the charter, they'd not be resuming a fruitless chase; now he meant to lose them in short order.

He came off the ridge, descended into a winding gorge, cut off into the first cross-canyon. Here it was all sheer travel over naked rock that left no sign. Missou worked roughly east through a tortured labyrinth of gorges, holding his bearings between the steep walls by the sun. Finally he emerged into an off-tapering of gentle sand hills. Confident that he'd shaken pursuit for good, he continued to swing west, now in a wide circle which he judged should bring him out on the straight road connecting town and Lionclaw headquarters.

He had ridden out the previous weary night getting Owen Rutledge, lashed to his saddle, safely into Blanco. Most of that time Owen had slumped unconscious or babbled in first delirium, but Missou remembered vividly his last rational words: "You see to Cissie M'Kandless; help her."

Missou had seen the girl only briefly on that day when Owen had braced Ivy North to save her father; he had taken away a swift impression of her youth and shyness and inexperience. If her uncle was all Owen had said, she'd need help badly. But Reed M'Kandless had had many hours to plan his move, and Missou could command only a near-despairing hope that he wasn't too late.

An hour's hard-driven pace across rolling country brought Missou out on the well-rutted Lionclaw main road. He promptly turned due west, guessing he wasn't more than three miles from the ranch headquarters.

The road was heavily bordered with tangled clumps of ocotillo and ironwood. Missou came to a dead halt at a strange, low sound from a thicket. He cantered his mount across the road and down a brushy aisle, hand on gunbutt and ready for anything. He caught the sound again and distinctly: a low, pain-tight voice little more than a broken whisper.

"Over here, son—over here."

Missou turned his head and saw him not twenty feet distant—a lean, long-faced man lying on his back beneath the thicket's edge. His head was raised, face twisted with pain. Missou dismounted, snatching his canteen from the saddle, and ran to the man. He stooped, lifted his head.

The man drank, leaned his head back with a sigh against Missou's supporting hand.

"Heard your horse. Too weak to look—but had to take chance you was a friend."

"My name's Holbrook." Missou frowned at the man's blood-soaked shirt.

"Dirksen . . . Paul Dirksen. Segundo at Lionclaw." Dirksen's hand clamped with a startling reservoir of strength on Missou's shoulder. "Boy, you got to save her . . . got to. . . ."

"Take it easy. You mean Miss M'Kandless by chance?"

"How—you know?"

Missou busied himself opening Dirksen's shirt as he answered. He undid the blood-plastered cloth tied around the body, winced at sight of the undressed wound beneath a wadded bandanna. Then he held Dirksen half-erect to ease off the man's shirt and tear it into strips for a fresh compress and bandage. Again Dirksen's hand caught his shoulder. "No time—for that. I got the strength to see to it. Say you're Owen Rutledge's friend?"

"That's right." Missou added as he carefully drew Dirksen deeper into brushy shade, "What's this about Miss M'Kandless?"

With jerky haste Dirksen told how, after leaving Lionclaw with his crew, he had deliberately fallen behind the others halfway to town, headed back for the ranch. Never having trusted the colonel's brother, he had anticipated Cissie M'Kandless' danger. But with a not-then serious wound pumping blood at each movement, he'd shortly been forced to dismount and rest. In so doing, he had lost a stirrup and fallen heavily. While he lay stunned, the animal had drifted away. Dirksen had tried to walk, but passed out from the effort. Coming to, he had crawled into the roadside brush and waited through half-conscious intervals for someone to come by.

About a quarter hour ago, he'd heard the approach of riders. He had fought to his knees to peer through the brush screen. He'd made out Fitz—an injured crewman who hadn't left Lionclaw with the others—and Cissie

M'Kandless coming along the road toward town. Abruptly Fitz had halted and pulled a gun. They were still too distant for Dirksen to hear their speech, but Fitz had forced Cissie off the road at gunpoint. The two were soon lost to sight across the wild range to the south.

"Fitz's a mean 'un," Dirksen whispered. "I make it he was hired by her uncle to do away with the girl. Don't know what Reed has brewin', but. . . ." His voice sank and trailed away.

Missou rose, studied the man on the ground. "You're one tough old rawhider. Held out this long. Think you can make it a while longer?"

"Never mind . . . you find them. Stop Fitz. But take care. Mean 'un. . . ."

"Be back soon's I can."

Without more words, Missou went to his horse, leaving his canteen by Dirksen. For the segundo's sake as well as the girl's, Missou prayed that Fitz hadn't gotten far.

He quickly found where they had left the road, and he followed up, tracking easily from the saddle. Their mounts' hoofs had left deep conical depressions in the sandy ground amidst the desert vegetation that laced this desolate, unused strip of Lionclaw range. A perfect place to murder a young girl. . . . Once he had picked out the line of trail, Missou moved fast.

He heard the gurgling flow of a creek before he came on it. Cutting east and west across the heart of Lionclaw, it was a swift deep current which no horse would ford. The tracks turned east along the steep cutbank, which Missou followed. He drew in hard at the first sound of voices ahead. They came from a clump of young willow trees lining the cutbank.

Missou swung down and slid on his hunkers down the cutbank. Its high slope would cut him off from an above view. He loped crouching, gun in hand, along the water's edge, and sank down a few yards from the voices, listening with held breath.

"Fitz," the girl was pleading softly, "let me go. I'll

leave Blanco Basin. My uncle will never know what happened, and you'll still get your money."

"You'd talk, you big bitch, blab it all over. . . ." The man's voice was slurred with pain and liquor and weakness, and Missou thought: *He's out of his head and about on his last legs.*

She said desperately, "But I swear—!"

"Girly," Fitz interrupted in a husky, wicked whisper, "What makes you think old Fitz don't *want* to kill you?"

Missou's palms were clammy with the knowledge that his first shot must be accurate, clear of the willows fringing the bank. He had to get almost beneath Fitz. He rose to edge farther up the bank. He saw Fitz's head and upper back, but not the girl.

"Accident, girly," Fitz went on, almost crooning it. "I'll jis' bust your neck with a few good stiff swings of this here gun . . . throw your carcass over the bank. Hoss threw you, see? Accident. . . ."

Missou suddenly straightened, bringing his gun up. The shift of weight to his heel crumpled the moist earth; to keep his footing Missou floundered back into the water. His foot plunged from the shallows into a drop-off and he fought for balance, caught it with a wild splashing.

Fitz was already turning, his six-gun arcing tightly around with this body. Missou flung forward and down as Fitz's gun roared. Missou lay on his belly with his upper body clear of the water and now he lifted his gun at the end of his extended arm as Fitz, cursing, stepped to the edge of the cutbank to shoot down. His narrow, vicious features cleared the rim, Missou gently moved his arm to fix the sights, firing on the instant.

Fitz's head rocked with the impact which flung him back from sight. Missou scrambled to his feet and up the cutbank. He half-climbed, half-fell over it—and stopped on his knees, sheathing his gun. The slug had taken Fitz, asprawl on his back, under the jaw and ranged up through the top of his skull. Missou felt his stomach lurch, set his teeth, and got to his feet.

The girl leaned against a willow tree, hands covering her face, shoulders shaking. With a soft moan she turned against him, burying her face in his shoulder. And Missou let a solicitous question die unspoken, and held her, wordlessly and awkwardly.

―――――――

SEVENTEEN

Tempered to hard times, Owen's bull-like constitution needed only a few hours of sleep and rest to begin the healing. He was jarred to a few fuzzy, pain-filled rational moments when the doctor went after the bullet embedded in his shoulder, and then he passed out. He came achingly awake to the distant voices of Virginia and the doctor conferring by his bedside, afterward slept again, soundly.

It was full dark when he blinked awake once more and became drowsily aware of where he was. He saw a lamplit crack beneath the bedroom door. "Miss Gilchrist."

His voice came as a parched whisper; he cleared his throat and called again. Virginia's quick footsteps came and she opened the door, paused there slimly silhouetted against the parlor light before moving to the cot. Her cool fingers touched his cheek. "You're feverish, try to rest some more. . . ."

"No." His voice was strong, his mind fought against the pain that throbbed afresh at his first movement. "Where's Missou?"

She was silent and he could not make out her face, but guessed that she was debating how much to tell him. Then she did speak, clearly relating how Missou had brought him here, hidden him and then tolled Claiborne out of town, though she'd had to bluff off two of his men. When she lapsed to silence, he said impatiently, "Well?"

Her shake of head was a weary little gesture. "I don't know. He promised to come back tonight. He hasn't come. But neither have Claiborne and his men returned . . . and your friend had a fresh horse. That's all I know, honestly."

"He tell you what happened before?"

She nodded mutely.

Owen dropped his head against the pillow, not looking at her, coldly berating himself for telling Missou to bring him here, placing her in this danger. A hurt and hunted animal's first instinct was sanctuary; in that same instinct he must have felt that no one but Virginia Gilchrist would give him sanctuary. Yet why turn to this prim and sheltered girl when only impersonal or bitter words had passed between them? And there was McVey, he reminded himself wearily.

"You know . . . I caught up with your friend?"

"Charlie?" she said in a small voice. "Yes. I know." Even as his lips formed apology, regret, she spoke quickly, yet painfully. "Don't, please. I know what your reason was—yet there must have been more to it—than Abner."

He stirred his head in a nod, looked back at the dark ceiling.

"I made arrangement for Abner's burial," she went on gently. "But listen, Owen . . . there was nothing more than casual friendship between Charlie and me. Not that, perhaps. We quarreled before you came—that night."

His gaze sought her half-seen face. "You want to hear why I was after him, why he killed Ab?"

"Yes—very much."

When he had finished, Virginia spoke quickly with a warm glad note to it. "I knew you had to have a reason, a just reason. I don't know how, but I knew." She sobered then. "But a terrible reason too . . . to follow three men all these years—"

Owen felt a hot lift of wrath. "They deserved it. And more. I wish I could make them pay all over. A hundred times over—"

"I don't mean that!" Her vehemence matched his own. ". . . What this has done to you—dedicating your life to a thing of hate. That isn't right. You can't go on this way forever!"

"Don't intend to," he muttered. "No longer'n it takes to get Cushing Tierney."

Virginia abruptly knelt by the cot. "Let him go, Owen." The angry response that trembled on his lips was dissipated by wonder for the desperate, pleading intensity of her. "Somewhere you have to make an end of it. Why not here? Let the authorities have him. If you don't . . . you're lost."

He wanted to snap that she was talking nonsense, but somewhere in his mind a nagging voice had long been telling him the same thing. He would kill Tierney, the last of the five who had murdered his family—and what then? The single purpose that had motivated his life for seven years would be finished, done. He would be, as Virginia said, a man lost, without hope or anchor. He had given Missou Holbrook good advice—*a man needs a reason*—and now in bitter clarity reared the stunted ugliness of his own central purpose, the reason he'd almost used up.

If there was a forked road in a man's life where only sheer will power could stay him from a wrong turn, he, Owen Rutledge, had reached it. He had to change before he lost even the will to change. Like young Holbrook, he was the kind of man who needed more than workaday existence and creature comforts to go on living; Virginia had seen this clearly. For a moment he almost hated her for that clear insight that made him face himself. It prompted him to lash out bitterly.

"What do you know of life? Even out here you've lived like a hothouse flower, insulating yourself in your comfortable past. And feelings? You don't have any. Except to get something for nothing, like that Rivera grant—"

Even as he spoke Owen felt a lurch of shame; if not for Virginia's instant courage, he'd be dead now. But he wasn't prepared for the stinging lash of her reply:

"What do *you* know of my past? You, born into a well-to-do family, good society, attending fine schools. You had every chance, now see yourself—rotted out with hate and revenge. *My* people were already bankrupt when I was born . . . oh, but a man wouldn't understand, men like to rough it. They leave the women to weep over the worn-out clothes they have to sew and re-sew, the family possessions they have to sell to keep a small larder filled, the drunken whining fathers they have to support. But then my father was sick—that was always his excuse—"

She bent her face against the cot, sobbing quietly. Owen touched her shoulder, murmuring tiredly that he hadn't known and fervently wishing he were elsewhere.

Her voice came muffled and broken: "You were right —about my feelings. I'm cold. Even Charlie McVey had said so. I don't want to be that way—I don't!"

"It's all right."

"No, it isn't!" She raised her tear-streaked face. Dimly seen, it looked wide-eyed and lost, like a little girl's. "I —I suppose everyone who's known nothing but poverty dreams of being rich. But most of them outgrow it—find happiness in what they have, like those poor people in Mextown. But that silly charter gave me a hope that made me shut out everything else."

"Times in some people's lives," Owen said gently, "when they've used up everything but hope. You had that right, Virginia."

"And what has my hope done? Brought a blood-thirsty gang after you and that boy, forced you to kill a man, almost got you killed. And God knows where that boy is, what's happened to him—"

Owen moved his hand gently, absently, on her shoulder, thinking grimly of Missou. Of Cissie M'Kandless too. If Missou had eluded Claiborne, he'd probably head for Lionclaw to help the girl, as Owen remembered telling him. The boy and girl both were in danger . . . and he and Virginia, too.

"We'll have to get out of here."

"But you're—"

"Now," he said inexorably. "This place isn't safe. Claiborne'll be back. You won't bluff him as you did his men."

"Can you walk?" she asked anxiously.

"I've got to." With the support of her arms and shoulder, he heaved to a sitting position, teeth set against the pain, and next to his feet. He closed his eyes against a wave of gray dizziness, took a few steps. "Let go," he told Virginia, and as she stepped away he started walking, setting his weight with infinite care on each step.

He moved out to the little kitchen while Virginia went ahead to light a candle on the kitchen table. Owen surveyed the pantry shelves, said, "Pack a grubsack. Some blankets. We'll make a camp a ways out of town. I'll get the horses, come back here for you." He smiled. "And don't forget your charter."

"Maybe if we left the charter for Claiborne—"

"Too late for that. He'll be like a mad wolf on the trail by this time. Nothing less than our lives'll satisfy him. If he finds us—"

"Can you make it to the stable?" She came nearer to him, watching his face worriedly.

"Sure." He took a careless step to prove it, at once lost his balance. Virginia caught at him and they swayed together off balance. His arms went around her as his hip struck the table edge painfully, and, "Oh Lord," Virginia gasped.

A current of air from the open window guttered the candle flame. As it sank and died, his head tipped down and in the dark his lips found hers. Unbelievingly he felt the firm small body melt against him without resistance, her mouth clung to his with a seeking, desperate passion.

He moved her away at last, breathing heavily. He touched her face lightly, awkwardly let his hand fall. "I'll be back fast as I can," he said huskily. "Now don't think about this, just hurry, get your things together."

EIGHTEEN

Owen moved carefully down the main street boardwalk toward the livery stable, holding to the gallery shadows, pausing often to rest his good shoulder against a building façade as his eyes raked up and down the near-deserted street. His wound blazed astir from its throbbing ache to flashes of wrenching pain that made him swallow against nausea. The night held a chill. His sheepskin was thrown over his shoulders; even that slight weight was an added discomfort. He kept his hand on his gun, grateful for a good right arm.

He reached the livery, turned into its wide archway, and paused to scan the lighted runway, seeing nothing of the hostler. He opened his mouth to hail the man, but stopped at the first sound of grouped horsemen moving upstreet from the north end of town.

He gave the street only a fleeting glance—saw the four riders coming abreast—stumbled deeper into the stable, his heart racing hammerblows against his injured shoulder. Claiborne had returned, and his first stop would be the stable.

Owen lurched into an empty stall piled with loose hay. He shrank between the stall partitions and hastily arranged a mound of straw over his legs and body. Lying prone, he drew more above his face, not enough to obscure his vision. He eased out his pistol and cocked it.

Motionless and scarcely breathing, Owen watched the four drooping riders, Claiborne in the lead, file past not two yards distant. They moved out of his sight; he heard their leather-creaking dismount. Claiborne roughly called for the hostler. Owen heard the man emerge from the rear office, begin a surly complaint which he swiftly choked off. Owen had only glimpsed the four but they were plainly hard-ridden, tired, and angry. He heard the hostler lead off the horses, then the men's low-voiced conversation.

". . . wasted too much time trying to find the kid," Claiborne said between his teeth. "Then got separated in those canyons, didn't find each other till nearly dark. Meanwhile that girl and Rutledge are probably laughing up their sleeves at us . . . with good reason."

"I told you—" began one man in a low, edged drawl, but Bloody Matt cut him off savagely.

"Just shut up, Blaize. I should have thought before sending *you* to search her place . . . but I've had time to think—most of a dirty sweaty day crawling through heat and brush and rocks. Rutledge was seen going with the Gilchrist girl to her house the very day he arrived in Blanco. I hazard that she hired him to find out who stole her precious charter. And we know that Clay wounded Rutledge when he and the kid broke past us last night. Of course the kid took Rutledge to her house! Where else would they go?"

"Blaize wouldn't make no kind of real search of the place this mornin'," rasped a vindictive voice.

"Of course, Danny," Claiborne murmured. "That's my point exactly."

"If that's so," Blaize drawled softly, "waste of time goin' back there. They've had time to clear out, go into hidin'."

"Maybe. Maybe not."

"Maybe not," Blaize echoed gently. "But you so much as touch that lady . . ."

There was a hiss of gunmetal clearing leather. "I've had about enough of your misguided chivalry, my friend," Claiborne declared harshly. "Now—we are going to pay a call on the lady. My gun will be trained on you the while. Move out!"

Owen watched the four move past toward the archway, Blaize tramping sullenly ahead of Claiborne's leveled pistol. Owen waited till they reached the street. He sheathed his gun and raised his good hand to grasp the stall partition. With a steady tugging pull he inched to his feet, stepped into the archway, his gun palmed again. A twist of his shoulders shed the bulky sheepskin.

There was no choice now. Half-dead on his feet, he couldn't skirt the rear of the buildings and reach Virginia's before they did. But could he take four of them?

It could be done. It had been done. In Wichita a year ago, he'd seen a half-dozen toughs choose a youth named Masterson. When the smoke had cleared, the six sprawled dead or wounded; Masterson walked away unhit. Afterward Owen had bought him a drink, asked him a question. *I had an edge,* Masterson had said. *A desperate man has got an edge.*

And now Owen could understand the cold truth of those words. There was no time to think of odds . . . no time to wonder whether his pain-wracked body could take the slam of his pistol's recoil.

He moved carefully erect to the archway, paused in its wide embrasure. The four were heading down the street. One favored his right leg, doubtless the man who'd wounded Owen and was in turn shot by Missou. The thickset man glanced idly back at Owen's steps. . . .

His shrill warning word halted the others, and they came about. Perhaps ten yards distant.

"Rutledge?" Claiborne called around the bobbing cherry-glow of his cheroot.

"All right," Owen said between his teeth. *Take Claiborne out first, the others may fold.*

"I feel generous, Rutledge . . . one final warning. You can't take all of us."

"I'll take you, then." Owen swung the cocked pistol up.

Claiborne flung himself sideways bellowing: "Scatter—spread out!" as his hand streaked for his gun. He hit the dirt on his side as Owen's weapon roared. It was a high miss; a store window behind Bloody Matt collapsed in a glassy jangle.

Owen lunged for shelter of the archway jamb, realizing in a cold detached relief that his body was numbly responding to the moment's desperate demand, awkwardly but painlessly. Claiborne was on his feet, running for a watertrough across the street. He lunged behind it as Owen fired again. The slug gouted a sparkling jet of water from the trough.

Blaize, too, faded back to the shelter of the watertrough, firing as he went. The small man called Clay limped toward another alley. The thick-bodied one, Danny, doggedly stood his ground with his short legs wide-braced, pumping bullets at the archway. Owen sank down in a tight crouch, hugging the wall. Slugs ripped through above his head, others furrowed into the clay floor. He heard Clay shout at Danny to take cover.

Owen stuck his head out for an instant, bore down and fired. Danny was lumbering toward Clay's alley, and now he pitched a few stumbling steps and fell across a tie rail. It split explosively beneath his bulk and dumped him in the dirt. He didn't move.

Claiborne and Blaize and Clay opened a concerted fire. Owen flattened out along the clay floor a second before the flimsy wall where he'd crouched was torn and riddled with slugs.

"Hold fire," Blaize called. "That must've got him. . . ."

Owen heard footsteps pound across the opposite boardwalk. He peered out and saw Blaize coming. The Texan caught Owen's movement and veered in his run, still coming on across the street. But toward a side alley.

Claiborne's exultant yell: "That's it, Blaize . . . get to the rear stable door, get behind him—"

Owen's arm jolted as he pulled trigger. And knew he'd missed; now Blaize was safely across, and cut off from his view.

Then farther downstreet another gun spoke. Blaize stumbled out to view again. He was hit, trying to bring his gun to bear on Owen's sudden ally, whom Owen in his prone position could not see. Blaize's shot merged with the unseen gun's second roar, and Blaize spun and went down on a knee—sprawled on his face soddenly. Saw the rider pulling up a fiddlefooting horse in the center of the street.

It was Missou Holbrook.

Owen did not wait now. He stepped out of the stable,

took two steps, and stopped as Matthew Claiborne reared up from the sheltering trough with a single baffled cry. He began firing at Owen, lifting his arm each time and bringing it down as though trying to throw each shot with a crazed violence. Owen's arm lifted and the sights hung steady and then he shot. Claiborne seemed to topple backward with slow trance-like grace. His gun clattered on the sidewalk boards. He fell out of sight behind the trough.

Owen only glanced at Clay as the small man threw his gun away and stepped out, hands high in mute token. Owen crossed to Claiborne and turned the body over with his foot. Paper crackled inside the dead man's bloody vest. Owen stooped and drew it out. Old and faded paper, the Armijo grant. Owen stuffed it in his pocket and trudged back to Missou who was off his horse and bending over Blaize's crumpled form. The boy glanced up, shook his head, and only then sheathed his gun.

"Something . . . this blooding of a man," he said shakily.

Owen said nothing, only shook his head and looked at Clay on his knees by Danny. The little man's ferret face lifted, meeting their stares with a bitter cold defiance.

"Danny's still alive. You'll finish it, I reckon. Go ahead. Make it both of us."

"He your partner?" Owen asked tonelessly.

Clay nodded.

"All right," Owen said very quietly and distinctly. "Get him to the doctor's. On your own, weasel-face. When he can ride, the two of you ride out."

Clay spat in his direction with one long look of unrelenting hate, and bent back to his friend. Owen's numb attention was pulled around by the rattle of a buckboard merging out of the lower street's darkness. He recognized Cissie M'Kandless on the high seat. Missou went to help her down. The girl was pale and exhausted, but unhurt, Owen saw with relief.

He stood nodding wearily as he listened to Missou tell what had happened. Townspeople began gathering about timidly in murmuring groups.

". . . went back to Lionclaw and got the buckboard to pick up Dirksen on our way in," Missou concluded. "He's in the wagon bed. Bad off, but alive."

Owen frowned, trying sluggishly to recall the question he wanted to frame. "Oh . . . you didn't see Reed M'Kandless—Tierney?"

"No sign of him on the place," Missou stated flatly. "No time to really look though, he might've seen us coming, lit out. . . ." He paused, peering anxiously into Owen's face. "Can you make it to Miss Gilchrist's?"

"I'm all right." Owen forced strength into the words. "You and Miss Cissie get Dirksen to Doc Hart's. Come on to the house after . . ." He felt the energy reserve that had sustained him swim away in a gray blur—felt the hot wetness crawl down his back. His wound had opened again.

Holding himself stiffly erect, he turned on a heel and went up the street. He saw a slim figure running toward him . . . her light dress a pale blur against the night. "Owen, Owen!" she sobbed. . . .

She had almost reached him when the shot came. Gunflame blazed from an alley to Owen's right. Owen felt a slug's whistling breath and turned with its sound, his gun out. There was a rush of retreating feet within the black areaway. Owen yelled hoarsely for Virginia to keep back. Again his mind swung back to urgent focus, held it tightly.

He went up the alley, walking fast. He blundered against a trash can, moved around it and reached the yard at the other end, drenched in window light from the adjacent buildings.

He came stock-still. Reed M'Kandless, the breath sobbing wildly in his throat, stood on a box by the high board fence that enclosed the yard, trying clumsily to heave his stout body over it. The box buckled beneath his weight and he dropped his gun to grab wildly at the fence top. Its splintered edge gouged his fingers and he cried out and went down in a quivering heap. All his nerve was gone; he stared with a hypnotic fascination at the man towering above him.

Owen kicked his gun out of reach. "Wait long, Tierney?"

"I wasn't waiting for you," Reed whispered huskily. ". . . For Claiborne."

"The bargain went sour, eh? But you'd settle for me. Well . . . doesn't matter now, does it?"

"Owen."

Virginia's hushed, pleading voice behind him did not make him turn. He reached down and fisted a handful of Cushing Tierney's coat, dragging the sagging bulk upright against the fence. He jammed his gun against the man's soft throat.

In the back of his mind he was waiting for Virginia to object again. Her skirt rustled faintly and he heard her quick breathing—nothing more. She was leaving it in his hands now. The moment for which he'd prayed was here, crowding him to decision. Kill Tierney or have him turned over to the law. What was the law?—a cold and dispassionate machine, man-made authority that could not sit in judgment on this moment for which he'd waited these long years. He was the judge here, and the jury . . . and yet he hesitated and the verdict could not wait. It must be now. Or never.

"All right, Virginia. . . ." His breath sighed from his lungs and his fist unclenched, and Cushing Tierney sank down in a sobbing heap at his feet.

Somehow Missou Holbrook was standing by him, taking the gun from his hand; Owen turned and took one long step and felt himself falling, never seeming to hit the ground. And endless vault of blackness caught him up and bore him away.

There was a pinpoint of light at the end of that black tunnel and his mind climbed doggedly toward it, and his eyes fought open. He knew Virginia's room, and the small cot where he lay, and a familiar face hovering above him. It was all a little dizzy and remote, yet clear enough.

"Coming along, old-timer?" Missou asked cheerfully.

The light hurt Owen's eyes, and he stiffly turned his

head on the pillow and saw with amazement high sunlight streaming mote-hazed through the east window.

"Lucky dog got his sleep," Missou observed with mock envy. "Doc Hart fixed you up . . . we-all have been waiting on you. Oh, Doc says Paul Dirksen'll pull through. Close thing with him."

His voice brought quick footsteps from the parlor; Virginia and Cissie entered. There was open relief and thankfulness in Virginia's face as she knelt by the cot, her eyes never leaving his face.

"Hope you settled that damnfool property by now," Owen whispered light-headedly.

Virginia's smile was tender and tolerant. "We have, sir. I'd be happy to tear up the charter—but Cissie insists that the four of us share alike."

"Four . . . us?"

"Well—we found the Armijo grant in your pocket . . . couldn't think who else it might belong to. There's my grant, too, and Cissie, as the colonel's only heir, also has a valid claim." She spoke lightly, yet with a deep and sure meaning. "With three valid claims around, Cissie thinks it'll be simplest, and certainly most just, considering all that we owe you and Mr. Holbrook, if she has partnership papers drawn up to include the four of us in Lionclaw ownership. Then we could destroy those two old grants . . . they have caused enough trouble."

Owen looked at Cissie, seeing the still-numb grief behind her quiet smile. In these few days she'd come quickly beyond girlhood. Yet he saw her sideglance touch Missou with a kindling warmth.

"Boy," she said softly, "you do want in on this?"

"Boy, eh," Missou said grimly. "I make I got a good three years over you."

"But you never did say your name," Cissie murmured contritely. "That silly Missou, that's no name."

Owen chuckled. Missou swallowed, his face flushing and faintly outraged. "Martin. Martin Holbrook. And I don't need any presents."

So Missou had found his reason and had renewed his young dreams into a reality. And Cissie had a shining new knight to whom she might look up. It was as well, Owen thought wryly; his own armor felt fairly tarnished. Cissie looked at him and at Virginia, and she took Missou's arm. "Come along, Martin, and we'll argue about presents."

When they had gone, Virginia was silent for a time, her hand absently stroking his forehead. She said at last, almost reluctantly, "Missou locked Tierney in a warehouse down the street . . . he's taking him to the Territorial Marshal's office at Santa Fe." Her eyes held dark and uncertain on his. "Owen, you did mean to let him live, didn't you? It was no mistake."

"Head was clear enough, I knew what I was doing," he answered gruffly.

Her face, warm and glowing, leaned close to his. "You did fight him, didn't you? And won?"

"His nerve gave out. No credit of mine."

"I didn't mean Tierney. Owen Rutledge was the man you had to fight. I had to know," she said gently, "that you had beat him," and her lips came to his in a soft rush.

66-8-3

ONE OF THE GREATEST WESTERN EPICS OF ALL TIME . . .

STAGECOACH
by ROBERT W. KREPPS

Based on the famous story by Ernest Haycox

The desperate ride through desperate country of an Overland Stage with nine star-crossed souls aboard

BUCK, *the driver*
DALLAS, *the dance hall girl*
DOC BOONE, *the drunkard*
HATFIELD, *the gambler*
MRS. MALLORY, *the lady from back East*
PEACOCK, *the whisky drummer*
CURLY, *the marshal*
GATEWOOD, *the banker*
RINGO, *the outlaw*

SEE THE TWENTIETH CENTURY-FOX MOTION PICTURE

A Martin Rackin Production
Starring
**ANN-MARGRET   RED BUTTONS
MICHAEL CONNORS   ALEX CORD
BING CROSBY   BOB CUMMINGS
VAN HEFLIN   SLIM PICKENS
STEFANIE POWERS   KEENAN WYNN**

k1667   40¢